NECESSITY

David Brunelle Legal Thriller #16

STEPHEN PENNER

ISBN: 9798218194338

Necessity

Joy Lorton, Editor.
Cover design by Nathan Wampler Book Covers.

THE DAVID BRUNELLE LEGAL THRILLERS

NECESSITY

Necessity is a defense to a charge of murder if

(1) the defendant reasonably believed the commission of the crime was necessary to avoid or minimize a harm;

(2) the harm sought to be avoided was greater than the harm resulting from a violation of the law;

(3) the threatened harm was not brought about by the defendant; and

(4) no reasonable legal alternative existed.

If you find that the defendant has established this defense, it will be your duty to return a verdict of not guilty.

State of Washington
Pattern Criminal Jury Instruction 18.02

CHAPTER 1

He almost made it outside.

Homicide prosecutor David Brunelle stood over the dead body lying face down across the threshold of the home's entrance. The corpse's legs were on top of the wooden floorboards of the foyer. His arms and head were splayed out on the concrete of the front porch. His back was riddled with bullet holes.

"I think we can rule out self-defense," Detective Larry Chen quipped from the opposite side of the victim.

Chen was a large man, a bit taller than Brunelle with a barrel chest and strong jaw. He was about the same age as Brunelle, mid-40s, but his style was a little old school, still wearing a sports coat to work when most of the younger detectives were wearing jeans. It worked for him, though. When Chen walked into a crime scene, everyone knew who was in charge. He had been dispatched as soon as the 911 call came in. It was his day to be on call. It was also Brunelle's turn to be the on-call prosecutor, so he was the one who joined Chen once the detective confirmed with his own eyes that it was a murder scene.

Brunelle nodded. "That's good. I'm sure the defense

attorney will think of something else. They always do."

Brunelle was in a suit because he'd come straight from his office at the courthouse. Lawyers were the only ones left in Seattle who still wore suits, it seemed, and even then he'd adopted the prevailing trend of loosening the tie a bit and undoing the top button. His short-cropped hair was beginning to gray at the temples. When he walked into a crime scene, or anywhere, everyone knew he was a lawyer.

It wasn't the first time the two of them had been called out to work a homicide together, and it probably wouldn't be the last. But this was different from those others in one notable way. It wasn't 2:00 a.m. in some downtown back alley. It was 9:30 a.m. in a nice residential neighborhood. The sun was shining and the air was filled with the sounds of birds chirping and children playing at a nearby school, not police sirens and distant gunfire.

Chen squinted down at the body and frowned slightly. The victim was a young man, early 20s, with short black hair and a couple days of stubble on his blanched face. He was dressed in a flannel shirt and jeans, brown leather shoes on his awkwardly angled feet. His hands were outstretched toward the road, but there was no weapon near them. By all appearances he was on his way for a morning walk, probably to the nearest hipster coffee shop.

"I'm looking forward to hearing that story," Chen said. "Six shots to the back. There's no way that's not murder."

Brunelle could hardly disagree. But he knew the defense attorney would. That was their job.

"So, who's our victim?" Brunelle asked. He glanced back inside the home. "Did he live here?"

"Caleb Hirsch," Chen identified the dead man. "He was renting this place with his girlfriend, Zoey Addison."

The house was a small, one-story ranch—the prevailing style when the city started growing in the 1960s. Half the houses in the city were probably one-story ranches. This one was in the Wedgewood neighborhood, on the other side of Interstate-5 from the University of Washington. It was the sort of neighborhood you might move to after you finished your degree, but then couldn't afford to buy a home with it. Although hardly anyone could afford to buy a home in Seattle anymore. Wedgewood was like most of the city's neighborhoods, filled with rentals, passive income for people fortunate enough to buy their homes twenty years earlier.

"Did the girlfriend see anything?" Brunelle asked.

"Oh, yes," Chen answered with a dark grin. "She's the one who shot him."

CHAPTER 2

Zoey Addison was smaller than Brunelle had expected. And more distraught than he would have wanted. He was glad the jury wouldn't see her in her current state.

She was seated at the dining table next to the kitchen, two uniformed patrol officers standing behind her on either side. She had a mess of wavy brown hair that brushed the tops of her shoulders, and dark eyebrows knitted together above large brown eyes. Tracks of mascara-tinted tears cut down her face. Her mouth was twisted into an almost grotesque frown of despair and horror. She didn't look like a murderer.

"Is he going to be okay?" she croaked as Chen and Brunelle walked into the room. "He's going to be okay, right?"

She didn't sound like a murderer either.

"He's not going to be okay," Chen answered. "He's dead. Because you killed him."

Addison dropped her blotched face into her shaking hands. "Oh my God. Oh my God. I didn't have a choice. I had to stop him. Oh my God."

"Stop him from what?" Brunelle asked. He could already

tell that was going to be the crux of the case.

Addison looked up again. More tears, more smears, more blotches on that sympathetic face of hers. "From killing those kids."

Brunelle nodded ever so slightly at the response. It was already getting worse. They needed to slow down.

"Let's back up," he suggested. He looked to Chen. "Can we start at the beginning?"

"The beginning is always the best place to start," Chen agreed. He gestured for Brunelle to sit down at the table, then sat down himself opposite Addison.

"But before we get started," the detective said, "I need to advise you of your Constitutional rights. You have the right to remain silent. Anything you say can and will be used against you in a court of law. You have the right to an attorney and have the attorney present during any questioning. If you cannot afford an attorney—"

"Oh my God!" Addison interrupted. "Am I a suspect?"

"You've already admitted that you shot him," Brunelle reminded her. "Yes, you're a suspect."

Addison took a moment, that small fact seeming to dawn on her for the first time. She nodded. "Okay, yeah. That makes sense."

"May I continue?" Chen interjected. "If you cannot afford an attorney, one will be provided to you at no expense. You can decide to exercise these rights at any time and not answer any questions. Do you understand these rights?"

Addison stared at Chen for a long moment. "Yes," she finally said.

"And with these rights in mind," Chen continued, "are you willing to answer my questions now?"

Another hesitation, but then another "Yes."

And they were off.

"Let's start at the beginning," Chen directed. "That man outside, Caleb Hirsch, how did you know him?"

"He's my boyfriend," Addison answered, not yet transitioning to the verb tense necessitated by her actions.

"Did you two live here?" Chen continued.

Addison nodded. "Yes."

She sniffled and rubbed the back of her hand across her nose. Basic questions with easily recalled answers weren't just a good place to start an interrogation; they also helped the subject of the interrogation to calm down. Focusing on small things made it possible to ignore the one really big thing: being under arrest for murdering your boyfriend.

"How long have you lived here?"

Addison had to take a moment to think. Another opportunity for her mind to distance itself from the horror visible just around the corner.

"Not very long," Addison answered. "Like six months maybe. I'm not exactly sure." She glanced around haphazardly. "I could probably find our lease agreement if you need that."

Chen shook his head. "No, that's okay. We can figure out the exact dates later if that becomes important. How long were you dating?"

Chen had no trouble using the proper verb tense. Hirsch was dead when he met him.

"Um, like a year and a half," Addison answered. She seemed almost embarrassed by the answer. She rubbed the back of her neck and looked away as she delivered it. "It was kind of on-again, off-again, you know? But we were trying to make it work. *I* was trying to make it work."

Brunelle frowned. He didn't like the sound of that. It made Caleb seem like the bad guy. Juries didn't like it when the murder victim was the bad guy.

"Were there problems in your relationship?" Chen asked. It sounded like concern. It wasn't. He was probing for a motive.

"I mean, yeah, I guess." Addison shrugged. "But like, everybody has problems, right?"

Brunelle knew that was true.

"But maybe we had more than typical," Addison ventured.

The dead body on the front porch supported that conclusion.

"Anything physical?" Chen followed up. If she was going to claim Battered Woman's Syndrome, this was her opportunity. But she didn't.

"No," she answered with a shake of her head. "It was all verbal. Emotional. Fucking with your head type stuff, you know?"

Again, Brunelle thought he did. Although maybe not to the extent Addison was talking about.

"Tell me," Chen encouraged.

Addison shrugged. "It was just, he could be really emotional, you know? Like, not just emotional. Emotions are fine, healthy even, right? But his moods could just change so fast, and get so extreme. Just when I thought everything was cool, he'd just start tripping about something. Like really bad, too."

"How bad?" Chen encouraged.

"Yelling, throwing things, punching the walls," Addison answered. "We had to buy a wall repair kit at the hardware store because he punched a hole right through the drywall. Twice."

That was bad, Brunelle had to agree.

"But he never hit you?" Chen confirmed.

Addison shook her head. "No, no. It was never like that. I mean, I locked myself in the bathroom a couple of times when it really got bad. But he always apologized afterward, and he never laid a hand on me. We never hit each other."

So, there would be no prior domestic violence reports, Brunelle considered. *And no medical records*. Chen asked the next question.

"Did he ever get any mental health treatment?"

Another shake of the head. "No, I don't think so. He probably should have. I kinda think he was maybe bipolar. Or maybe even borderline. He was definitely depressed sometimes. And then lately he just started getting really, really paranoid. But he didn't want to go see anyone about it, and I was scared to suggest it."

That meant no mental health records either. And Zoey Addison's amateur psychological diagnosis was unlikely to provide a legal justification for summary execution.

"What happened this morning?" Chen moved on. If it wasn't a chronic motive, then it was a specific motive.

Addison's eyes glassed over again. The questions that focused away from the actual murder had allowed her mind a brief respite. The break was over.

"So, the paranoia thing started to get really bad." Addison opted to give some more background first. "He started talking about the cops and the feds and like secret, deep-state operatives and stuff I didn't even understand. He said they were watching him. That's why he started buying the guns."

"Guns?" Chen asked.

Plural, Brunelle noted.

Addison nodded again. "At first it was just one. I wasn't super comfortable with a gun in the house, but he said it was for protection. He kept it in a lockbox and it's not like we have kids or anything, so I didn't want to start a fight about it. But then he got another one. And then another one. And another and another."

"Handguns?" Chen asked.

"Yeah," Addison answered. "No rifles or anything. I don't know a lot about guns, but I went to the shooting range a few times with my dad growing up. One of them was a revolver, but the rest were semi-automatics. He kept the revolver in the lockbox, but just started leaving the rest all around the house. He called them his 'drop guns'. In case someone surprised him inside the house, he said. Or in case we had to run away without time to grab anything else."

Undiagnosed paranoid schizophrenic with a house full of loaded guns, Brunelle considered. *What could possibly go wrong?*

"So, what happened this morning?" Chen directed Addison back on track.

Her face contorted again and she took a minute to respond. "He'd started talking about the school up the street," she said. "About how schools are really government buildings, and the kids are just there to hide what's really going on. Like when terrorists hide inside hospitals, he said. He said they weren't even really neighborhood kids. They were the kids of the agents working at the school. The ones watching him."

"That's concerning," Chen admitted.

"I know!" Addison exhaled. "I told him it was crazy. I mean, I didn't use that word because, well, I thought it might set him off. But I told him he was wrong. They were definitely neighborhood kids. I mean, we see them at the store and the park and stuff. At first he argued with me, but then all of a sudden he agreed with me and told me he was just stressed out from work and everything. So, I dropped it and he didn't bring it up again."

"How long ago was that?" Chen asked.

Addison thought for a moment. "About a week ago. Maybe a week and a half."

"And nothing about secret agent school kids watching him?" Chen asked.

"No, nothing," Addison confirmed. "Nothing until this morning."

"What happened this morning?" Chen asked for the third time.

Addison's damp eyes widened and she cocked her head slightly as she looked at Chen and answered. "He was so calm. That's what was so scary. He just sat up straight in bed and said, 'That's it. Today is the day.' I didn't know what he meant, so I asked him, 'The day for what?' He said, 'Those kids. Today is the day. I let them think they fooled me, but they didn't fool me, and today I'm going to show them I know the truth. I know what they're doing. I know who they really are. They aren't innocent, and they're going to pay.'"

Brunelle frowned, for a lot of reasons.

"Then he pulled the covers off of his side and got out of bed," Addison continued. "He didn't say anything else. He just started getting dressed. I asked him what he was talking about, but he wouldn't answer me. Then he grabbed the gun off his nightstand."

Brunelle's frown deepened, for all the same reasons.

"I got out of bed and told him to just calm down and tell me what was going on," Addison continued, "but he just said, 'They're not innocent, Zoey.' Then he looked me right in the eye and asked me, 'Are you innocent?' It scared the shit out of me. I'd never seen him look like that before, even with everything else that happened. And he had that gun in his hand. I didn't say anything. I just froze. He said, 'I thought so', and then walked toward the front door.

"I didn't know what to do, but then I remembered those kids. He was going to kill those kids. I just knew it. So, I ran after him. I grabbed him and told him not to do it. I told him to just stop for a second and sit down and maybe we could call a doctor or something and they could help him. Honestly, I thought he might shoot me right then and there, but I had to do something. But he didn't shoot me. He didn't even point the gun at me. He just ignored me. He pulled his arm away and headed for the front door.

"I screamed at him to stop, but he just pulled on his shoes and unlocked the deadbolt. I didn't know what else to do but then I saw one of his guns lying on the table by the door. I grabbed it and pointed at him and told him to stop or I'd shoot him.

"He stopped and turned around to look at me, but I don't think he thought I'd really do it. My hands were shaking. 'Just stop, Caleb,' I said. 'Put the gun down and let's call a doctor.' But he didn't say anything. He just shook his head and turned back to the door. He pulled it open and I yelled at him to stop or I would shoot him. He hesitated for a moment, then raised his own gun and racked the slide. I yelled, 'Stop!' one more time, but he didn't stop. He started out the door. He was going to the school. He was going to slaughter those kids. I didn't have any choice."

She dropped her face into her hands.

"I shot him," she gasped between sobs. "I killed him."

Brunelle sighed. At least he knew what he was up against.

CHAPTER 3

"Sounds like she's a hero," opined Brunelle's girlfriend, Casey Emory, after he recounted the interrogation to her over lunch.

"Remind me to strike you from the jury," Brunelle replied. "And anyway, that was just her version of events. Everyone's the hero of their own story."

"That sounds like a motivational quote," Casey observed. "Or maybe a pop psychology explanation of why people act the way they do."

"Or the reason why the jury shouldn't believe her," Brunelle suggested. "You can't just go around killing people."

"You can if they're going to kill a bunch of kids," Casey argued. "If he'd made it onto the school grounds with a gun and the security guard shot him dead, that guard would definitely be a hero."

Brunelle frowned and took another bite of his burger. "I just think," he said through a half-full mouth, "that there must have been other options."

"Easy for you to say," Casey replied. "You're a man."

"What's that supposed to mean?" Brunelle said.

"It means, check your privilege," Casey replied. "You haven't spent your life smaller than everyone around you. Less powerful than everyone around you."

Brunelle frowned at that. "It's not like I'm some giant. Six-two, a hundred-ninety pounds isn't that big."

"Six-one," Casey countered with a chuckle, "and hundred-ninety-five. And yes, that's big. Plus, you're a dude. And you're White. You're used to people doing what you say, just because you say it."

"I'm not sure what my race has to do with it," Brunelle defended.

"And if you were a Black woman like me, you would," Casey responded. "So, listen to me. It's easy for you to think she had an alternative because you would have had one. If you'd told him to stop, he would have had to at least consider the possibility of a physical fight with you, and losing it."

"Why, thank you." Brunelle straightened his tie.

"But not everyone on the jury will feel that way," Casey pressed ahead. "There will be people on that jury who will know that her words were never going to be enough. You have to think about it from her perspective, and that perspective is looking up at a man with a gun."

"That all assumes she's telling the truth," Brunelle pointed out, "and didn't just shoot him in the back because he was leaving her."

"I suppose that's true," Casey allowed. "So, did Larry arrest her?"

"Oh, definitely," Brunelle confirmed. "You don't admit to shooting someone to death and not get arrested for it, no matter how good your explanation is."

"So, he didn't buy it either?" she asked.

Brunelle shrugged. "I'm not sure," he admitted. "Parts of it were pretty compelling. But a little too convenient, if you ask me. I guess he thought so too. At least enough that he wasn't going to just let her walk out the door."

"Well, not with that dead body in the way, anyway," Casey quipped.

"Exactly." Brunelle pointed a French fry at her.

"So, arraignment tomorrow?" Casey continued. "You are going to charge her, right?"

Brunelle hesitated.

"What?" Casey asked, over her own plate of fries. "A second ago you were all righteous indignation and fiery retribution. Did I get in your head?"

Brunelle grinned. "You're always in my head, honey. But no, that's not it. I want to be a hundred percent sure. I'm going to see what the medical examiner says before I decide."

"When's the autopsy?"

Brunelle checked the time. "Right after lunch."

Casey winced and pointed at Brunelle's burger. "And you got ground beef?"

Brunelle shrugged. "It's not like I haven't seen a dead body carved up before."

"Still, I'm impressed," Casey offered. "And not just by your iron stomach. I think it's good you want to have all the information before you decide what to do."

Brunelle accepted the compliment with a nod. "Thanks. It's a big decision."

Casey smiled sideways at him. "Speaking of big decisions…"

Brunelle dropped his remaining lunch on the plate. "Oh,

look at the time," he said, standing up. "I don't want to be late for my autopsy."

Casey shook her head and laughed. "It's not your autopsy, dummy. But it will be if you keep avoiding the topic. You can't say yes to the big question, then refuse to answer all the little ones that make it possible."

"I don't know." Brunelle stepped around the table and kissed Casey goodbye on the cheek. "It seems to be working so far."

CHAPTER 4

There were, generally speaking, four categories of evidence. Eyewitness testimony. Expert opinion. Photos and videos. And physical evidence. The autopsy combined all those. An expert doctor would tell the jury his opinions based on his firsthand observations of the victim's dead body. With pictures.

Brunelle arrived for the autopsy a little after 1:00. He would have until the next morning to decide whether to charge Zoey Addison with murder. He was pretty sure he was going to do it, but the last thing he wanted was to make that decision and be unpleasantly surprised by the pathologist's findings. Addison's claims were going to be difficult enough to overcome. Expert opinion in favor of innocence would be one obstacle too many. Plus, that kind of evidence would mean she was probably innocent and he wasn't supposed to prosecute probably innocent people.

"Dave!" the medical examiner called out when he arrived. "Great to see you again."

Brunelle reflected for a moment on the strange variety of people he'd gotten to know because of his career. Had he pursued a different path, he likely never would have met someone like Dr. Peter Jacoby, and he knew his life would have been poorer for that.

Dr. Jacoby was what they used to call 'a tall drink of water.' He was four inches taller than Brunelle and probably twenty pounds lighter, with a shock of hair on the top of his head that was blond when Brunelle first met him but had turned mostly gray since then. But all the years of spending his days intimately connected to death hadn't diminished his passion for life. Brunelle wasn't sure he could say the same for himself.

"Hey, Pete," Brunelle returned the greeting. "How's the woodworking class going?"

Jacoby's face lit up, pulling the skin into well-worn smile-wrinkles. "You remembered! It's going great. I just finished my first cutting board."

Brunelle didn't actually care about Dr. Jacoby's hobbies, but he knew he was supposed to engage in small talk before getting to business, and he recalled the good doctor mentioning being excited about trying out that new woodworking class the last time Brunelle had imposed on him to observe an autopsy.

"That's great," Brunelle offered. Then he gestured toward the examining room and the dead body on the table inside. He was done with the small talk. "Speaking of cutting…"

Jacoby took a moment, then burst out laughing. "All right then! Let's get started." He gestured at Brunelle's attire: dark suit, white shirt, red tie. "It looks like you've got court after this. Better not dawdle."

Brunelle did not, in fact, have court after the autopsy; he was just supposed to wear a suit every day. Brunelle acknowledged the comment with a friendly grunt and they headed inside the examining room.

"You know, my mother always wanted me to be a lawyer," Jacoby remarked as they made their way to the table upon which rested the remains of Caleb Hirsch. "She was very disappointed when I decided to go to medical school."

Brunelle was surprised by that. "She was disappointed you were going to be a doctor? Isn't that the stereotype of what every mother wants?"

"She also wanted me to be a stand-up comedian."

Brunelle cocked his head at him. "Really?"

"Yeah."

"Wow."

"Yeah."

Caleb Hirsch was lying face up on the examining table. He was still in the blood-soaked clothing Brunelle had observed on the porch that morning. Part of the autopsy was examining the clothing before removing it. If there were six bullet holes in the clothes but only three in the body, that was a problem. Jacoby set to examining the garments, and Brunelle took up a position to the side, close enough to see what Jacoby was doing, far enough to not be in his way.

There didn't appear to be any ground-shaking observations on the clothing. The holes in the clothes lined up with the holes in the body underneath. Jacoby noted a lack of singeing or sooting at those holes, consistent with Addison being several feet away when she fired. The real surprise came when Jacoby removed the clothing and they could observe Hirsch's naked body in its entirety.

"Are...?" Brunelle pointed up and down the length of the body. "Are those bruises?"

Jacoby took a step back to observe and pushed a hand through that thick gray hair. "They sure are."

And there were a lot of them. All up and down his arms, his legs, ribs, and chest. Purple and green and yellow and brown spots covered the body like the spots of a cheetah. A cheetah that ran into things a lot. Or got hit a lot.

"Those are pre-mortem, right?" Brunelle knew the answer. It was a stupid question, actually, but he couldn't help himself from asking it.

"Bruises form from blood escaping capillaries after blunt force trauma," Jacoby said. "That doesn't really happen after the heart stops beating. And they definitely don't heal after death."

The various colors marked the levels of healing. The deep purple ones were fresh; the yellow ones were the oldest. Hirsch had plenty of both, and every color in between.

Brunelle pointed at the menagerie of injuries. "You're going to document all of these, right?"

"Of course," Jacoby confirmed. "You think these are more important than the gunshot wounds?"

Brunelle nodded. "She admitted to the gunshots."

CHAPTER 5

"She beat the shit out of him."

Jessica Edwards, public defender and Brunelle's opponent once again, frowned down at the paperwork he'd provided her upon their arrival at the arraignment court the next day.

"The declaration for probable cause says she shot him," Edwards said. "Is that not accurate?"

"No, that's accurate," Brunelle answered. "But before she shot him to death, she was beating the shit out of him. He was bruised from head to toe."

Edwards shrugged. "Maybe he played rugby on the weekends. Or he was just really clumsy and walked into things a lot."

Brunelle shook his head. "Maybe he was finally leaving her and she shot him in the back on his way out the door."

"That's your theory of the case?" Edwards scoffed. "A woman spurned?"

"Hell hath no fury, right?" Brunelle countered.

Edwards rolled her eyes. They were in the main criminal

courtroom of the King County Courthouse in downtown Seattle. It was the courtroom where they did the arraignments all afternoon, every afternoon. The judge hadn't taken the bench yet, but the courtroom was filled with prosecutors and defense attorneys, with a couple of jail guards standing sentry at the door to the holding cells tucked behind the courtroom. It was the same thing as every other day and yet still full of energy. Routinely frenetic.

"Your so-called victim was about to shoot up a school playground." Edwards held up that probable cause declaration again, the document where the detective summarized the facts that formed the basis of the charges. "My gal is a hero."

"You sound like my girlfriend," Brunelle frowned.

Edwards cocked her head slightly. "Trouble in paradise?"

"Nah." Brunelle brushed the suggestion away. "She just likes to disagree. It's recreational. If I'd said I wasn't going to charge it based on your client's bullshit story, she'd say I was going soft and needed to hold a murderer responsible."

"You are going soft," Edwards teased, "but that's good for me."

Brunelle was about to ask her what she meant by that, but the bailiff interrupted the attempt with a call to attention.

"All rise! The King County Superior Court is now in session! The Honorable Kevin Rogers presiding."

Brunelle had appeared before Judge Rogers more times than he could remember. He was a solid judge with a solid reputation. The arraignment would go smoothly and he could get back to figuring out why Edwards thought he was going soft.

"Are there any matters ready?" Judge Rogers asked. There were a couple dozen arraignments on that afternoon, all scheduled at 1:00 p.m. But each had a different pair of prosecutor and defense attorney. A new judge might try to force their way through the docket in alphabetical order, only to find that case after case was missing either one attorney or the other as each of them had to attend to several different cases at once. An experienced judge surrendered to the chaos and accepted the cases as they came to them.

"The *Addison* matter is ready, Your Honor," Brunelle announced. He nodded to the guards across the courtroom and they set to the task of retrieving the defendant from the holding cells. Brunelle and Edwards stepped forward to take their temporary spots at the bar before the judge. A few moments later, Addison entered the courtroom and took her position next to Edwards. She was dressed out in red jail scrubs and one-size-fits-most plastic slide shoes. Red meant high security. Murder defendants were always high security, even if she didn't look dangerous. And she didn't. She looked even smaller in the baggie scrubs, and her eyes looked even bigger as they gazed around the busy courtroom.

"This is the matter of *The State of Washington versus Zoey Claire Addison*," Judge Rogers stated for the record. "Are the parties ready to proceed to the arraignment?"

A lot of court hearings were really just formalities, but formalities could be important. The purpose of an arraignment was to advise the defendant exactly what they were accused of. Edwards couldn't defend Addison if she didn't know what the charges were. Brunelle had already given her the charging documents, so the only thing to do on the record was acknowledge as much. And then argue bail.

"The defense acknowledges receipt of the complaint," Edwards informed the judge. "We waive formal reading and ask the Court to enter a plea of not guilty to the charge of murder in the first degree."

"A plea of not guilty will be entered," the judge confirmed. And the arraignment was over. Time for the bail hearing. "Do the parties wish to be heard regarding conditions of release?"

The answer to that question was 'Of course,' and Brunelle went first. The prosecutor almost always went first.

Again, it was a formality. Brunelle hoped so anyway. Bail on a Murder One was usually a million dollars. Sometimes more, almost never less.

"The State asks the Court to set bail in the amount of one million dollars," Brunelle said. "The defendant is charged with murder in the first degree. She is facing a very lengthy prison term if convicted. The State believes she is therefore a flight risk. In addition, the victim in this case was her boyfriend and she shot him in the back. Accordingly, we think she might pose a risk to other members of our community. Bail is appropriate and one million dollars is a reasonable amount under all of the circumstances. Thank you."

The only problems for Brunelle were that the case wasn't actually as routine as all that, and Edwards wasn't one to rest on formalities.

"Ms. Edwards?" the judge invited her response.

"Thank you, Your Honor," Edwards answered, then launched into her argument. "The State has elected to charge my client with the crime of murder in the first degree, but that doesn't mean she did it. To the contrary, she is presumed innocent of that charge and in fact, committed no such crime. Mr. Brunelle cherry-picks the fact that my client was forced to shoot her boyfriend in the back, but he conveniently and intentionally leaves out the reason why."

Edwards placed a supportive hand on her client's shoulder. "The reason why she had to shoot her boyfriend—the man she shared a home with, the man she loved—was that she had no choice. Caleb, the alleged victim, was suffering from mental health issues and going through an especially bad and dangerous episode that morning. He had picked up one of the many handguns he had stashed around their home and announced that he was going to walk across the street and start murdering school children. Zoey begged him to stop, but he wouldn't listen and he opened the front door, intent to commit not just one murder, but dozens, and of the most innocent souls.

"My client was faced with a choice. A terrible, awful choice. But really, there was no choice. She did the one and only thing she could do to protect those children. She stopped her boyfriend. That's not murder. That's necessity. She isn't only presumed innocent, Your Honor, she is innocent. She never should have been charged and the Court should release her on her own recognizance so that she can properly and fully prepare her defense against these unfair charges. Thank you."

Judge Rogers raised an eyebrow ever so slightly. "You want me to P.R. a murder defendant?"

Edwards raised her chin. "Yes, Your Honor."

Rogers nodded and turned to Brunelle. "And you want me to set bail on someone who, at least by her attorney's account, saved the lives of scores of school children?"

Brunelle raised his chin slightly as well. "That story is the defendant's version of events. The State disagrees."

Judge Rogers nodded and harumphed to himself under his breath. "There is a very large gap between a million dollars bail and zero dollars bail," he observed. "But I suppose that gives me a lot of room to find a middle ground. Ms. Edwards is correct that her client is presumed innocent, but Mr. Brunelle is correct that neither the State nor this Court are required to accept a defendant's version of events at face value. There is probable cause for the charge. Whether a jury decides there is proof beyond a reasonable doubt is yet to be seen. I am not going to let a murder defendant walk out without posting bond, but neither am I going to treat this like any other murder that has come before me for arraignment. This one is different, and I think you know that, Mr. Brunelle."

Unfortunately, Brunelle did know that.

"I am going to set bail in the amount of five-hundred-thousand dollars," Judge Rogers ruled. "That concludes this matter."

The guards moved in quickly to extract Addison before she even had a chance to ask her lawyer what the judge's ruling might mean for her release. Brunelle and Edwards knew.

"I guess we both lost," Brunelle quipped as they stepped away from the bar.

Edwards shrugged. "I lost more. Today, at least. My client can't post five hundred thousand any more than she could post a million. But I think I might have been the winner long-term."

Brunelle's eyebrows knitted together. "What do you mean?"

"If Judge Rogers thinks there might be something to my defense," Edwards explained, "just wait until I get in front of a jury. You're not going to be able to just rely on the same arguments you make at every murder arraignment."

"Is that what you meant by me getting soft?" Brunelle returned to the topic.

But Edwards demurred. "Oh, no. No, I was just kidding. You're not going soft, Dave. You keep doing exactly what you're doing. Don't change a thing."

That was the last thing Brunelle wanted to hear from an opponent. Edwards took her leave and Brunelle took a moment to consider. If he was going soft—that is, if he was buying Addison's story even a little bit and relying on the same old, tired arguments—he was going to need someone to kick his ass into gear. Especially if he was going to go home every night to someone casting doubt on the righteousness of his prosecution.

"Carlisle."

CHAPTER 6

"I'm in."

Brunelle hadn't even had a chance to knock on Carlisle's office doorframe.

"I haven't told you about the case yet," he responded.

"Doesn't matter," Carlisle answered. "It's been months since I've been in trial. Everybody keeps pleading guilty."

"That's what happens when you get a reputation as a kick-ass prosecutor," Brunelle observed.

Carlisle frowned. She was seated at her desk, jacket draped over the back of her chair, a pen in her hand and a very thick case file open in front of her. Her blonde hair was cut a little shorter than Brunelle last remembered, just below her jawline, and her blouse looked new too. She looked like she was ready to step in front of a jury to deliver an opening statement.

Dress for the trial you want, Brunelle supposed.

"I don't know about that," Carlisle demurred, "but I'm happy to piggyback onto your apparently less than kick-ass reputation if that means you've got a case that's going to go out to trial."

Brunelle grinned at the jab. "Yeah, I'm pretty sure it's going to trial."

"Good." Carlisle gestured at her guest chairs. "Tell me the facts, and why we're going to win."

So, Brunelle sat down and did just that. Or at least the part about the facts. He was still working on how they were going to win exactly.

"So, she's a fucking hero," Carlisle scoffed.

"That's what Edwards said," Brunelle recounted.

Carlisle frowned. "It's Jessica? Ugh, of course it's Jessica."

"You don't like her?" Brunelle was a bit surprised. He'd always gotten along with her, even in the heat of trial.

"I'm indifferent to her as a person," Carlisle answered. "But she's a good lawyer and juries like her. She'll be able to sell the hero angle."

Brunelle couldn't disagree. "Not if we blow it up."

"How do we do that?" Carlisle questioned. "Our victim sounds like a nutjob."

"We might not want to say that in our opening statement," Brunelle laughed. "And maybe we can keep Edwards from saying it too."

"How?"

"We prove it wasn't true," Brunelle answered. "We get his mental health records."

"Didn't our killer say he wouldn't go to therapy?" Carlisle pointed out.

"She did say that," Brunelle agreed, "but I'm not about to believe some murderer."

CHAPTER 7

Realistically, they couldn't just contact every mental health counselor in Seattle and ask if Caleb Hirsch had been a client. And none of those providers would have told them anyway. Patient confidentiality. A subpoena could get around that, but they'd need to identify the specific therapist before they could fight that battle. Caleb Hirsch was in no condition to tell them who his counselor was. Fortunately, in addition to the autopsy and arraignment, there was another proceeding that was standard at the beginning of any murder case. Meeting with the victim's family.

There were almost countless variations of families, including no family at all. That one was the easiest. No meeting and no expectations. The hardest was the close-knit, sobbing family, fairly begging for a conviction as if that might bring back their loved one somehow. Most of them were somewhere in the middle, with maybe some family members crying and others stoic. Caleb Hirsch's family was small, apparently, or at least the ones who could be bothered to meet with the prosecutors after his murder. The only person who met with Brunelle and Carlisle that morning was Caleb's father, Gerald. He wasn't sobbing. He didn't act stoic either. He just seemed tired.

"Thank you for meeting with us, Mr. Hirsch," Brunelle shook the elder Hirsch's hand.

Hirsch's grip was average, not too strong but not weak either. That described most of him actually. He was probably just under six feet tall, although it was hard to tell for sure because he held himself with a sort of permanent slouch. His hair was graying but not all gray yet. He wasn't overweight, but he had a bit of a paunch. His clothes were various earth tones, a little too big for him, and topped with a windbreaker that he didn't bother to take off indoors.

"Thank you," Hirsch returned with a shrug. "I'm not sure what good it'll do."

Brunelle appreciated that attitude. It would make the meeting easier. He could never promise a conviction, but that didn't keep family after family from asking him to.

"We're here to answer any questions you might have, Mr. Hirsch," Carlisle spoke up as they took seats around Brunelle's desk. She was in another brand-new suit. Brunelle was starting to feel underdressed around her.

"Is she going to plead guilty?" Hirsch asked. "Zoey, I mean. She killed him, right?"

"She did," Brunelle confirmed. "But she's not going to plead guilty."

"She's claiming she had no choice," Carlisle put in, "because of your son's mental health issues. Any insight you might have regarding that could prove very valuable."

Hirsch sighed. "Well, Lord knows Caleb had a lot of issues. Mental health issues, I mean. They started when he was a teenager. At first, we thought it was just the usual high school stuff, but it was more than that."

"Who's 'we'?" Carlisle asked.

"His mother and me," Hirsch explained.

"Is she...?" Brunelle started, not knowing if perhaps she was dead.

"She's still around." Hirsch understood the hesitation. "But after a while, she couldn't deal with it anymore. She just left. We're still married, but only because it's not worth the trouble of divorcing. We haven't seen each other in person for a couple of years now. She left it to me to deal with Caleb."

Brunelle didn't mind the backstory, but he didn't find it particularly interesting either. He would only need one witness to identify the photograph of Caleb Hirsch. Gerald Hirsch would be perfectly adequate. But he did want to know more about Caleb's problems.

"What were you left to deal with?" he asked.

"Caleb," Hirsch answered, "or rather, what Caleb started turning into. He was always a sweet little kid. Kind and funny. He made friends easily and all of the teachers loved him. But then he started changing. Like I said, at first we thought it was just the usual teenager stuff, and some of it probably was. He stayed in his room all the time. He stopped talking to us. His grades plummeted. He didn't seem to have any friends. It was really difficult. It's really difficult to see someone you love suffer like that."

"Did you ever seek professional help for him?" Brunelle asked. That was going to be the most useful information for their case.

"Yes," Hirsch answered, "and a bit to my surprise, it worked. Of course, by then, Betsy had left, so I was the one who had to convince him to go. It was easier than I thought. I don't think he liked being miserable either. We found a really good psychiatrist and they were able to help him. It wasn't a cure, but it was a treatment. I got some of that sweet little boy back."

Brunelle nodded. The jury was going to eat that up.

"Zoey," Carlisle interjected. "His girlfriend. The one who killed him. She said he never got treatment."

Hirsch shrugged. "I don't know about never. He might have stopped, but he saw a therapist all the way through high school. He started dating Zoey after he graduated. I think they matched on one of those dating apps, but I'm not totally sure. I met her a couple of times. She seemed nice enough. I don't know. At some point you have to let your children grow up. He knew how important his mental health was. I'd be surprised if he just stopped getting the help he needed."

"When was the last time you saw him?" Brunelle asked.

Hirsch frowned. "Well, I had to identify the body, if that's what you mean."

It wasn't. "No, I mean when did you last see him alive?"

Hirsch nodded and took a moment. "We had a standing date for lunch once a month. We were due for another one when I got the call from the detective about, well, about what happened. I guess we should have met early that month."

Gerald Hirsch seemed like a very nice man who had very much been beaten down by life. He didn't appear so much sad about his son's death as exhausted by it.

"What was your son's diagnosis?" Carlisle asked. She wasn't one to dwell on the importance of keeping loved ones close, or whatever. There was a case to be won.

"They said it was probably a personality disorder," Hirsch answered. "I remember them saying paranoid personality disorder or maybe borderline personality disorder. They also said he was presenting as at risk for schizophrenia, but they didn't think it was that. At least not yet. Apparently there are medications for schizophrenia, but the personality disorders are actually harder to deal with, in a way. They did something called dialectic something or other."

"Dialectical behavior therapy," Carlisle said.

"Yeah, that's it." Hirsch pointed at her. "I don't know how much good it did. It was a lot and he didn't like it too much. I wouldn't be surprised if he stopped going. That's probably what led to all of this."

Brunelle frowned. He didn't want Hirsch to say that in front of the jury. "Regardless of your son's efforts to maintain his mental health, he didn't deserve to be killed."

But Hirsch just shrugged.

"What was the name of the last doctor your son saw?" Brunelle asked. They could use that information. Especially because Addison said Caleb wasn't seeing anyone. Another lie.

"Jennifer Kilgrove," Hirsch answered. "Over on Forty-fifth. I think she's connected to the university somehow."

Even better, Brunelle thought. Clinical psychiatrist with the University of Washington. Instant credibility boost. Maybe she was even a professor.

"Thank you, Mr. Hirsch." Brunelle was ready to end the meeting if his guest was. "Is there anything else we can answer for you right now?"

Hirsch smiled slightly, but darkly. "I don't think you have the answers to the questions I really have, Mr. Brunelle. But I appreciate that you have a job to do anyway."

CHAPTER 8

"What do you think he meant by that?" Casey asked.

They were at Brunelle's condo, lounging on his couch after a dinner of takeout from that amazing Taiwanese place downtown. She had her head on his lap and he had a bourbon in his hand.

"I'm not sure," Brunelle answered. "Probably just stuff like life and death and justice and the futility of all human existence in the face of the inexorable march of time and entropy."

Casey laughed. "Oh, is that all?"

Brunelle shrugged. "I just heard that he appreciates the job I'm doing."

"That sounds about right," Casey replied. "It's always about you, huh?"

"It's sometimes about me," Brunelle insisted.

"Is it ever about us?" Casey grabbed the initiative.

Brunelle stifled a sigh. "Of course, darling. It's always about us."

"Except when it's about you," Casey teased.

"Even then," Brunelle knew to say.

"Have you given any more thought about which place we should move into?" Casey asked, pulling his drink-free arm around her. "I like your location, but my place is bigger."

"Yeah," was all Brunelle responded.

After a moment, Casey lifted her head up. "Yeah? Nothing more?"

"Yeah, you're right?" Brunelle tried.

Casey sat all the way up. "You're not getting cold feet about moving in together, are you?"

"Of course not," Brunelle insisted. "There's just a lot of details. And you know how it is. After a long day of dealing with other people's problems, the last thing I want to do is face my own."

One of Casey's eyebrows shot up. "Moving in together is a problem?"

Oops. Brunelle set his drink down on the coffee table. He knew not to argue that point. "My place," he answered her original question. "We should move into my place. It's smaller, but there's only the two of us. It's closer in, and it will be easier to rent your place out to some nice young family who can't afford to buy a house in your good school district because housing prices on the West Coast are insane."

Casey's expression faltered. She was prepared to fight. He disarmed her. "Really?"

Brunelle considered for a moment then nodded. "Yeah. My place."

Casey nodded too. And smiled. "Okay, your place." She looked around. "Our place."

Brunelle picked his bourbon up again. "So, can we talk about my case again? With futility and justice for all?"

"Go talk to that psychologist," Casey advised. "I bet she

confirms everything your defendant said. I'm telling you, she had no choice. She's innocent."

"I'm not sure this living together is going to work if you don't support me in my work," Brunelle told her.

"Your work is justice," Casey replied, "and sometimes justice means a 'not guilty' verdict."

"Says the cop," Brunelle pointed out.

"Says the human being," Casey returned. Then she pointed at the wall above the couch. "Enough about you. I think I want to take down that photo of the Seattle skyline and put that painting I have of the California poppy fields right there."

That gave him two things he wanted to argue with her about. Instead, he took a long sip of his bourbon, savored its flavor for a few moments, then swallowed both it and his pride. "Yes, dear."

CHAPTER 9

Dr. Jennifer Kilgrove's office was in a converted house near the University of Washington, about a mile due north of the upscale 'University Village' shopping center. It was one of those areas of Seattle that the city council rezoned into light commercial, leading to the desired influx of dentists, acupuncturists, and counselors of various stripes. You could still imagine the 1950s 2.5-children family playing in the front yard if you squinted hard enough to ignore the large wooden business sign out front. Brunelle found a parking spot on the street in front of the daycare two doors down, and he and Chen exited his vehicle.

"I hope this goes smoothly," Brunelle said as they made their way along the sidewalk. "I'm not much in the mood for a fight today."

"Isn't that your job?" Chen questioned. "It's called the adversarial system for a reason, right?"

"In the courtroom, sure," Brunelle responded, "but I don't need fights in every other area of my life too."

Chen was silent for a moment. "And how is Casey?"

Brunelle laughed. Chen knew him well after all their years together. "Just working through the details of the move-in. It's fine. Everything is fine."

"Sounds like it." Chen rolled his eyes slightly. They had reached the entrance to Kilgrove's building. "After you, counselor."

Brunelle thanked his companion and pulled open the door. The interior had been remodeled to conceal the fact that it had once been a home. There was a waiting area where the dining room had probably been. There was a hallway to the offices that were once bedrooms. And the kitchen was now a file room, with a counter in front, at which was seated Dr. Kilgrove's receptionist.

"Good morning," the young woman chimed as they stepped inside. "Do you have an appointment with Dr. Kilgrove today?"

"I'm afraid not." Chen produced his badge. "I'm Detective Chen with Seattle Police. This is David Brunelle with the county prosecutor's office. We're here to talk to the doctor about a former patient of hers."

"He was murdered," Brunelle put in. He suspected she would be more helpful if the former patient was the victim instead of the murderer.

The woman looked appropriately shocked. She had probably expected another day of ADHD kids and depressed divorcé(e)s. "I, I'll see if the doctor is available."

She jumped to her feet and hurried down the hallway toward one of those bedroom/offices. A few moments later she reemerged. "The doctor can see you now."

"That was quick," Brunelle commented under his breath.

"I have that effect on people," Chen replied. "At least the good people of the world who aren't used to dealing with murder investigations."

Kilgrove's office was the first bedroom on the left, just past the bathroom with its bathtub and shower. Probably too expensive to remove, and maybe useful after an especially long day at the office. The office was decorated in the sort of typical office furniture one could acquire at the nearest big-box office supply store. A brown laminate over pressed wood desk, a fake leather desk chair, and two black guest chairs, only the seat upholstered. There was some sort of tree-like plant in the corner, and a view of the backyard out the window. It was the perfect size for a swing set.

"Thank you for meeting with us, Dr. Kilgrove," Chen began.

Kilgrove stood up to shake her guests' hands. She was in her late 50s, with gray streaks in her black hair. She wore simple glasses and a comfortable-looking sweater. Brunelle could imagine telling her his deepest secrets.

"Don't thank me yet," she said. "I'm not likely to be of much help, what with patient confidentiality and all that."

"Understood," Brunelle put in. "If it helps any, your patient was the murder victim in our case. He's not alive anymore to assert that privilege."

"I have obligations independent of my patients, I'm afraid," Kilgrove replied.

"Can you at least confirm Caleb Hirsch was a patient of yours?" Brunelle requested. "It would have been a few years ago. If you can do that much, I think we can take care of the rest."

Kilgrove frowned and sighed through her nose. After a few moments of thought. "I can confirm Caleb was a patient. Anything more than that, I'm afraid you'll need a warrant."

Brunelle nodded and turned to his partner. "Larry?"

Chen extracted his phone. "All prepped. I just needed that confirmation to establish probable cause. The judge is waiting." He pressed the send button on his email app. "This will only take a few minutes."

Kilgrove's eyebrows shot up. "Wow. I expected you'd have to come back in a week or two."

Brunelle shook his head. "Not anymore. We have a pretrial with the defense attorney next week. I'm going to need this information before then."

"Oh," was all Kilgrove replied.

"Would you like to hear what happened?" Brunelle offered. "You know, while we're waiting. You might find it interesting."

"I'm sure I will," Kilgrove agreed. "Would you like some coffee while we're waiting?"

"Fresh pot?" Brunelle asked.

"Keurig," Kilgrove explained.

"Close enough," Brunelle answered. "That would be great. I take mine black."

"Two creams, one sugar," Chen added.

Kilgrove picked up the phone and gave their orders to her receptionist. "All right then. What happened to Caleb?"

Brunelle told the story; Chen filled in some of the gorier details. Kilgrove listened with interest, but didn't say anything as the tale unfolded. Brunelle was watching for any cues that might give away her opinion as to how likely it was that Caleb would have acted in the way Addison claimed, but Kilgrove maintained her poker face impressively throughout the presentation.

"Does any of that sound plausible to you?" Brunelle asked when they had finished.

Kilgrove smiled politely. "Ask me again when you have

that warrant."

"Just got it," Chen announced. He offered his phone to the doctor. "Do you want to read it off my phone, or is there a printer I can send it to?"

Kilgrove frowned slightly at the screen, then relented. "The phone is fine. Just print out a copy before you leave for my records. Lindsey can help you with it on your way out. And to answer your question, yes, all of that sounds plausible. More than plausible. I'm not surprised by any of it. Saddened, but not surprised."

"His father told us Caleb's diagnosis was a personality disorder with a concern about schizophrenia," Brunelle said. "Is that accurate?"

Kilgrove nodded. "He had some indicators of schizophrenia, paranoid type, but not enough for a complete diagnosis. Often, schizophrenia appears in early adulthood, but it hadn't happened yet, so it made more sense to address it as a paranoid personality disorder. He also had pretty bad ADHD. He had a lot of challenges."

"Sounds like it," Brunelle agreed.

"We're going to need copies of all of your records." Chen remained matter-of-fact about their visit. "Is there anything you can tell us to help us understand those better?"

"I'm also interested if he went to see anyone after he finished with you," Brunelle added.

"He was supposed to," Kilgrove answered. "My specialty is youth and teenagers. I keep some clients into adulthood, but the stressors and societal expectations can be significantly different. I have a few colleagues I pass clients off to, depending on their individual needs."

"Who did you pass Caleb off to?" Brunelle asked.

"I'd have to look at the records," Kilgrove admitted. "It would have been either Emily Su because of the schizophrenia or John Young because of the personality disorders."

"The ADHD didn't matter?" Brunelle asked just out of curiosity.

"We finished our sessions when he graduated from high school," Kilgrove explained. "That made the ADHD a less urgent issue and more secondary to the others."

That makes sense, Brunelle supposed. Kilgrove called Lindsey again and requested Caleb's file. When it arrived, the doctor thumbed through to the end, then was able to announce, "Okay, I didn't refer Caleb to anyone immediately when he finished with me because he was doing well, but he contacted me again about six months ago, so I referred him to Dr. John Young. He specializes in personality disorders. I didn't have any information that the schizophrenia had manifested so I decided the focus should be on the personality disorders." She frowned. "It sounds like maybe I was wrong."

"Not necessarily," Brunelle consoled. "That story we told you, that was the killer's version. I, for one, don't believe it."

CHAPTER 10

It turned out to be more difficult to speak with Dr. Young than it had been to speak with Dr. Kilgrove.

"Dr. Young is out of town until next week," his receptionist informed Brunelle and Chen when they drove to his clinic in an office park in Seattle's Northgate area. There was a mall there of the same name, although Brunelle was pretty sure the neighborhood and the mall were both named after its location at the north end of the city, rather than the neighborhood being named after the mall. In either case, Dr. Young wasn't there. He was in Aspen for the week.

"Will he be back Monday?" Brunelle asked. His pretrial with Edwards was on Monday afternoon.

"Tuesday," the receptionist answered. He was a slight young man in his early twenties, dressed all in black. "We're closed on Mondays."

Of course, Brunelle grumbled to himself. Every weekend a three-day weekend and week-long ski trips to Aspen. He had chosen the wrong career.

"Don't worry about it, Dave," Chen counseled. "I'll get

another warrant. In-person this time. Old school. I'll have whatever records we need by the end of the day tomorrow."

"Warrant?" the receptionist croaked. "Records? Oh dear. Can't this wait until Dr. Young gets back? He's not going to like it if I give confidential records to the police while he's gone."

"That's the beauty of it." Chen grinned. "You're not going to give them to me. I'm going to take them."

* * *

And take them, Chen did. Young's complete file on Caleb Hirsch. He got them to Brunelle by Friday and on Monday, Brunelle marched into the pretrial conference and slapped them down on the table in front of Edwards.

"There!" he announced triumphantly. "Proof your client lied to the police."

Edwards looked up from where she had been sitting, peacefully reviewing a police report from one of her other cases while she waited for Brunelle and Carlisle. She looked from Brunelle to Carlisle, who just nodded, and back again.

"Okay…" Edwards picked up the stack of papers. "Excuse me for not taking your word for it. Do you mind if I look at these and see what the hell you're talking about?"

"Be my guest," Brunelle encouraged with a flourish of his hand. He crossed his arms and waited patiently for Edwards to review the documents, a confident grin on his face.

Edwards didn't read every word, of course, but she took long enough to understand what she was looking at. Once she had accomplished that, she set the records down again. "You realize this helps me, right? This actually confirms what my client said about your victim."

"Your client said he wasn't in treatment," Brunelle pointed out. "These records show that he was going right up until the end. He saw Dr. Young the week before your client murdered him."

"So, these records," Edwards tapped them, "show that my client was right about the diagnosis, but wrong about his current level of treatment. That means he really was capable of shooting up the school."

"She lied, Jess," Brunelle insisted on his interpretation.

"Or he did, Dave," Edwards offered hers. "I can easily spin this that he was hiding his treatment from her. Maybe he was embarrassed he still needed it. Maybe he was getting worse and didn't want her to know."

Oh crap, Brunelle realized.

"It doesn't matter if he was actually going to his therapist," Edwards continued. "It matters if she knew. You can't prove she did. Which means you can't prove she wasn't lying."

Brunelle's grin was long gone.

"That's not how I see it," he tried.

"It doesn't matter how you see it," Edwards almost laughed. "It matters how the jury sees it. And so far, I think they're going to see it my way."

* * *

The pretrial had not gone how Brunelle had expected. Those records were supposed to be the smoking gun. But Edwards wasn't denying there was a gun or that it was smoking. She was claiming the gun and the smoke were justified.

There was no deal to be made. Brunelle wasn't going to amend down from Murder One. Edwards wasn't going to plead her client guilty to it. All that was to be done was to confirm the matter for trial in 45 days' time. Enough time, Brunelle hoped, to be able to find concrete evidence that Zoey Addison lied to the police and killed her boyfriend for any reason other than the one she claimed.

"That could have gone better," Carlisle observed, once they were out in the hallway. "But it could have gone worse."

"Really?" Brunelle questioned. "How could it have gone worse?"

"We're pushing her to uncover her defense," Carlisle said. "We're locking her into a story. If we know exactly what she's going to say before trial, we can adjust our case to box her in."

"I don't know," Brunelle replied. "I feel like we're the ones in a box. And it's getting smaller."

"Hey there, you two!" A voice called out from down the hallway. It was Casey. Brunelle had a lunch date scheduled with her. He didn't realize it was so late already.

"Hey there, lady," Carlisle greeted Casey and she walked up to them. "Long time, no see. How goes the move-in?"

Casey raised an eyebrow at Brunelle. "Ask Dave. He's the one holding things up."

"I am not holding things up," Brunelle defended. "There's just a lot of decisions to be made. Gwen, what do you think should go over a couch: a painting of a landscape or a photograph of the city skyline?"

"Oh, no." Carlisle put up her hands and took a step back. "I am not getting in the middle of this. No way."

Casey laughed. "Smart." Then, "Hey, did you get a haircut? It looks good."

Carlisle reached reflexively to cover her hair. "What? No. I mean, yeah. I guess. I don't know. We've got trial coming up, so, you know I need to look good in front of the jury, is all."

"Trial is in a month and a half," Brunelle pointed out.

"That's going to fly by," Carlisle insisted. She gestured down the hallway. "Well, I guess I'll be going. You two enjoy your lunch or whatever. I'll see if I can't come up with some actual good evidence for us. Okay. See ya."

And she turned and walked briskly away.

"That was weird," Brunelle observed.

"Is she wearing a new suit too?" Casey asked, watching after Carlisle.

"I think so," Brunelle answered.

Casey grinned. "She's got a new girlfriend. And she works in the courthouse."

Brunelle was unprepared for that deduction. But before he could argue, Casey said something even more outlandish. "We should go on a double date with them."

CHAPTER 11

The only good thing about a proposed double date with Casey, Carlisle, and Carlisle's new romantic interest, was that it made paying a visit to a ski-loving part-time psychiatrist seem appealing in comparison. Brunelle had hoped the records would speak for themselves, but Edwards had shown she was more than willing to speak for them herself. That meant Brunelle would need Dr. John Young after all. Maybe the good doctor could put a counter-spin on whatever Edwards tried to do in front of the jury.

Chen came with Brunelle again for the second trip to Young's office. They had the records, so he wouldn't be needed to serve a subpoena, but Young was potentially going to be a witness at trial. That meant anything he said to them now had to be disclosed to Edwards right away. It also meant Brunelle would need a witness he could call to the stand in the unlikely, but not impossible event, that Young said something materially different when he testified. Materially different in a way damaging to Brunelle's case, that is.

"Hello again," Brunelle greeted the young man behind the reception desk as he and Chen entered the office. "Dr. Young is back from Aspen by now, right? Or did he extend his vacation?"

"I did not extend my vacation," Young himself announced as he emerged from a hallway on the other side of the waiting area, "but I was tempted. Twenty inches of fresh powder fell on my last day."

Young looked like the kind of guy who was successful enough to take every Monday off and go skiing at Aspen. He was late 40s, with a tan face, white teeth, and thick hair combed straight back from his face. He wore a sweater like Kilgrove had, but his looked expensive rather than comfortable. It flattered his muscular physique.

Brunelle wasn't much of a skier, but he knew enough people who were to reply, "That's a bummer." Then, "Dr. Young, I presume?"

Young confirmed his identity and offered a handshake to both Brunelle and Chen as they introduced themselves as well.

"Shall we go back to my office?" Young suggested. "I imagine you have some questions for me about Caleb."

They did indeed. And Young's relaxed attitude gave Brunelle one more.

"You don't seem concerned that we obtained Caleb's private psychiatric files," Brunelle observed.

"Concerned?" Young questioned. "Why would I be concerned? As soon as I heard what happened to Caleb, I knew the police would be coming by. I even had Evan make a complete copy of the file to give to you in case you came while I was in Aspen, which you did. Did I mention the powder?"

"You did mention it," Chen confirmed. "But I had to obtain a subpoena for the records," he pointed out.

"Well, of course you did," Young said. "And of course

you obtained it. And of course the records were ready when you did. It's not like there's anything surprising in there."

"Do you mind if we ask you a few questions anyway?" Brunelle asked. "It can be hard to learn everything important from chart notes."

"Of course, of course," Young answered. They had reached his office. "Please, sit down and make yourself comfortable." He tapped his phone to turn on some calming background music. "What wisdom can I impart to you?"

Brunelle looked to Chen. Chen gave him an 'after you' nod and took a seat in one of the chairs in Young's office. Brunelle took another, and Young sat down in his own, very nice, leather chair. Brunelle felt like he was in a therapy session.

"I guess my first question," Brunelle began, "is whether his girlfriend, Zoey, knew Caleb was coming to see you."

Young nodded. "Very good. Very insightful. Yes, that is an important question."

Brunelle nodded, waiting for an answer to his important question. None seemed to be forthcoming.

"So?" he prompted.

"So," Young echoed, "it's difficult to say. You need to understand that I have to rely on my clients' own reports as to what they do when they leave my office. Caleb told me he hadn't told Zoey yet about our sessions."

Brunelle frowned. That would mean she was wrong about Caleb seeing someone, but not lying.

"But that may not have been true," Young added.

Brunelle's hopes raised.

"But I think it was," Young concluded.

Those hopes crashed again. "Why do you say that?" Brunelle inquired.

"Because I think I would have heard from her," Young explained. "I usually hear from invested significant others, but I never heard from Zoey. That, plus the fact that Caleb reported he hadn't told her yet led me to the conclusion that he was being truthful about that."

"Is it a common problem," Chen inquired, "that your clients aren't truthful with you?"

Young smiled broadly, showcasing those white teeth of his. "Yes, I'm afraid it is. In fact, I often assume they're lying to me. Part of the goal of therapy is to get them to be open with me. But there's a reason that's a goal."

Brunelle supposed that made sense.

"Do you have any other questions about Caleb's relationship with his girlfriend?" Young asked. "It wasn't our only topic of conversation—it probably wasn't even our main one—but we did discuss it."

Brunelle did have a question about that actually.

"Did Caleb ever report any physical abuse by his girlfriend?" he asked. "The autopsy revealed a rather large number of bruises all over Caleb's body. I was thinking it might indicate he was a victim of physical abuse."

Young took a deep breath, then sighed it out. "I can't say for sure that there was no physical abuse. As I said, my patients aren't always completely candid with me. But those bruises, I think there may be another explanation."

Brunelle didn't like the sound of that. *But the truth is the truth,* he supposed. "What's the other explanation?"

"Self-harm," Young answered. "Cutting is the more popularly known version of it. But there are patients who will strike their bodies against objects, resulting in bruising."

"All over their bodies?" Brunelle found it hard to believe.

"Yes," Young answered. "Imagine being so angry that you punch something. We've all been there, right?"

Brunelle supposed he had. He nodded.

"Well, punching a wall is going to bruise your knuckles," Young said. "So will smashing your arm against it. Or your leg. Or imagine dropping to the floor and thrashing around like a toddler. Little two-year-old Timmy isn't going to do much to himself or the furniture, but twenty-year-old Tim might break the coffee table, and get several nasty bruises for his trouble. So, no, I don't think those bruises came from his girlfriend. Why? Did she admit to striking him?"

Brunelle shook his head. "No, it was just something I wondered about."

"It was a theory crafted by a lawyer," Chen added, "based on incomplete evidence. I have to deal with that all the time."

Brunelle threw a look at his friend. It said 'Really?' without saying, 'Really?'

"Also," Young added, "I would have expected him to record something like that in his journal, and I don't recall ever reading about any physical abuse from his girlfriend."

Brunelle and Chen looked at each other again. Brunelle turned back to Young. "Journal?"

"I assume you've read Caleb's journal by now," Young answered.

Brunelle turned and frowned at Chen. Chen frowned back.

"Did you find any journals?" Brunelle asked the detective.

Chen shook his head. "We searched the residence thoroughly. We didn't find any journals."

It was Young's turn to frown. "That's strange. Caleb was definitely keeping a journal. We would go over it in session."

"What was in the journal?" Brunelle asked.

"Probably not what you want," Young replied, nodding slightly. "Zoey's claiming self-defense, right?"

Brunelle wasn't surprised Young knew his client's girlfriend's name. She was probably a frequent topic of conversation in therapy.

"Not exactly. The defense is called 'necessity'," Brunelle explained. "She's not claiming he was threatening her life. She's claiming she had no choice in order to prevent an even greater evil."

"The school kids." Young nodded again.

Brunelle was surprised Young knew that part. Or rather, he was concerned. "You know about the school kids?"

"Caleb and I talked a lot about those school kids during our sessions," Young answered somberly. "Especially the last few. He was growing increasingly fixated on them."

That wasn't what Brunelle wanted to hear.

"Did he talk about shooting up the school?" he asked.

Thankfully, Young finally shook his head. "No. Not explicitly. Not yet."

"Not yet?" Chen questioned.

"Not yet," Young repeated. "We were still working on the nature and causes of his delusions about the school children. He hadn't voiced any plans yet regarding them, although I could tell that's where we were headed. He just wasn't ready to tell me yet."

"Maybe because he wasn't really planning on doing that," Brunelle posited, if perhaps a bit too hopefully.

"It would be nice to think so," Young allowed with a faint smile, "but it's unlikely, in my professional opinion. His journal would tell you for sure."

And suddenly Brunelle had a quest.

CHAPTER 12

"Journal?" Carlisle frowned at Brunelle. She turned to Chen, "Did you find any journals?"

Chen shook his head. "No. I know what's important in a murder investigation. If there had been a journal, we would have seized it."

They were seated around Brunelle's desk. The trip to Young had been productive. Brunelle wanted to share their findings with his trial partner, and plot their next steps.

"Let me see those records," Carlisle pointed to the ever-growing case file on top of the desk. "I want to see if Young ever references any journals."

"He references 'written work'," Brunelle answered as he slid the file across to her. "I checked. He never uses the term 'journal'."

"So, Edwards doesn't know," Carlisle observed.

"Not yet, but we have to tell her," Brunelle reminded her. "We can't hide stuff. That's not how it works."

"I know how it works," Carlisle snapped back. "I'm not

suggesting hiding evidence. I'm just waiting for her to do something. She's been too quiet. As soon as we tell her there's a journal and that journal is missing, we're going to be up in front of a judge fighting off a motion to dismiss for failure to preserve exculpatory evidence."

"We don't know the journal is exculpatory," Brunelle responded.

"Well, that's kind of the whole point," Carlisle returned. "Crazy guy writes in his journal that he's going to kill a bunch of school kids, then picks up his gun to go do it. Right now, we can claim Zoey Addison made all of that shit up to justify murdering her boyfriend because, who knows, he was leaving her or something equally clichéd. But if Caleb wrote it down himself, in advance, we're fucked."

An accurate, if profane, summary of their current position.

Chen pushed himself out of his chair. "I guess I better find that journal then. I'll have the boys sweep the house again. Maybe it's hidden in the floorboards or something."

"Good luck," Brunelle offered.

"If it doesn't help our case, pretend you didn't find it," Carlisle said. Then, when both men looked aghast, she laughed. "I'm joking. Do your job. We'll do ours. Yay, truth. Go, justice."

Chen shook his head slightly, but smiled, and took his leave.

"You think he'll find it?" Carlisle asked after the detective had left.

Brunelle wasn't sure. He said as much. "I hope so, though, if only because of what you said. If we can't find it, Edwards will use it as an excuse to try to dismiss the case."

"She doesn't need that excuse." It was Nicole Richards,

Brunelle's paralegal. She was standing in the doorway with a document in her hand. "Courier just dropped this off. A love letter from Ms. Edwards."

She handed it to Brunelle, who read the caption aloud. "Motion to Dismiss for Lack of Evidence. Necessity Defense. *State v. Knapstad.*"

"A *Knapstad* motion?" Carlisle scoffed. "On a murder case?"

A *Knapstad* motion was a challenge to the sufficiency of the State's evidence. It was named after the case that established the procedure. The defense agrees, for the sake of argument, that everything the prosecution alleges is true, then asserts that it's insufficient as a matter of law. The assertion is that no reasonable jury could possibly find the defendant guilty given all of the State's evidence and every reasonable inference therefrom. If the judge agrees, then there's no point to putting it to a jury and the case is dismissed. They were common motions on drug and property crime cases, but extremely rare in murder cases. They had a dead body with six bullet holes in its back. It would be hard to say no jury could convict on that evidence. But that was exactly what Edwards was saying.

"It looks like she's saying since the only version of events we have is the defendant's," Brunelle gleaned from his first quick glance through the pleading, "we have to accept that as true, and if what she says is true—"

"It meets the necessity defense, and she's not guilty." Carlisle could finish the argument. "It's total bullshit."

"Is it?" Nicole asked, still hovering over Brunelle's desk,

Brunelle frowned. "No."

CHAPTER 13

The hearing on Edwards's motion to dismiss was scheduled for two weeks out. Enough time for the State to file its response, which would consist of twenty pages of, '*Is too enough!*', with case cites and a few Latin phrases thrown in for good measure. It would also give Chen time to try to find that journal. Maybe the journal would show that Caleb Hirsch was doing well in therapy and not in fact plotting the murder of innocent school children. That would cast enough doubt on Addison's story to allow the case to proceed to a jury.

The problem was, Brunelle couldn't wait until the journal was located to tell Edwards about its existence.

"Journal?!" Edwards nearly choked on the word when Brunelle called to tell her. It wasn't an email conversation. "He was keeping a journal? When were you planning on telling me that?"

"Right now," Brunelle answered. "That seems kind of obvious actually."

Brunelle could hear Edwards sigh over the phone.

"You want to delay your motion to dismiss?" Brunelle

suggested. "There may be something in the journal that proves your client was lying."

"Or proves that she was telling the truth," Edwards countered. "Any chance you'll find it before the hearing?"

"I hope so," Brunelle answered. "Chen is working on it right now, so probably."

"Yeah, Larry is pretty good at that sort of thing," Edwards agreed. "I'm not going to move the hearing, but I may do some supplemental briefing, depending on what's in the journal."

Brunelle nodded. "Me too."

CHAPTER 14

Chen was pretty good at that sort of thing, but he wasn't perfect. No one was.

"Sorry, Dave," Chen reported two days before the hearing. "We looked everywhere, but we didn't find anything. I even checked for loose floorboards. Nothing."

Brunelle frowned. The worst scenario was that Chen found the journal and it supported Addison's claims. Something like, *'Dear Diary, I'm going to murder school children tomorrow morning.'* The second worst scenario was not finding it at all, because that would let Edwards argue it would have had that sort of entry and the prosecution intentionally, or even just negligently, lost that critical evidence of the defendant's innocence.

"Has anybody been in there since the murder?" Brunelle asked.

Chen frowned. "Yeah," he admitted. "After we processed it—and quite fully, I might add—we let family in to gather any personal items we hadn't collected as evidence."

"Whose family?"

"Both families," Chen answered. "First his, then hers."

"Did you monitor what they took?" Brunelle hoped.

"Me personally? No," Chen answered. "And by then, we had fully documented the scene and collected all of the evidence."

"Except the journal," Brunelle pointed out.

Chen shrugged. "Honestly, I'm not sure there really is any journal. Just because that doctor told him to do it, doesn't mean he did. If you were going crazy and thinking everyone was after you, would you really start writing things down?"

"I might if I were crazy," Brunelle answered.

Chen shrugged. "Fair enough."

Carlisle appeared then, stopping halfway through Brunelle's doorframe and frowning. "Did I miss the email about a meeting? Or are you guys talking about a different case?"

"No, it's the Addison case," Brunelle admitted. "And this isn't so much a meeting as Chen dropping by unannounced to tell me he struck out."

"No secret journal under the floorboards?" Carlisle surmised.

"Afraid not," Chen confirmed.

"Not even a still-beating heart?" Carlisle joked.

"What?" Brunelle had to ask.

Chen frowned at him. "Have you ever read a book?"

"I haven't read Caleb Hirsch's journal," Brunelle shot back, "because you couldn't find it."

Chen grinned. "Touché."

"I was thinking about that," Carlisle said. "In fact, that's why I came up here. What if the journal isn't really a journal?"

"That's deep, man," Brunelle said. "Is any journal ever really a journal? How many journals must a man journal, before we call him a man?"

Carlisle shook her head at him. "I'm serious. You guys are old enough to remember when calculators were invented. But Caleb and Zoey were kids. They grew up on smartphones and the cloud."

"What's the cloud?" Brunelle feigned ignorance, putting on an old man's voice.

"It's other people's computers," Chen answered.

"That's true actually." Carlisle pointed at Chen. "So, what if Caleb's journal was online?"

"Like one of those online document things?" Chen asked. "Cloud docs or whatever."

"I was thinking social media," Carlisle suggested. "Have we looked at his social media accounts?"

Chen frowned. "I should have done that."

"Never too late," Brunelle said. "Except we don't know his passwords. They're probably written down in his journal."

Chen stood up. "I'll get started on the warrants. Those big tech companies take forever to respond to warrants."

"Can you shorten 'forever' to like tomorrow?" Brunelle asked. "I'd love to have that stuff before the hearing on Edwards's motion to dismiss."

"I'll see what I can do," Chen replied.

"Any chance they fight the warrant?" Carlisle asked.

Chen shook his head. "Nah. They don't give a shit about anyone's privacy. Hell, that's how they make money, selling your information to advertisers. They just want a piece of paper to cover their asses."

"In the meantime, we can probably track down any public-facing accounts," Carlisle said. "See what he's been posting."

"Do you need an account to do that?" Brunelle asked.

Carlisle shook her head at him. "You dinosaur. Yes, and I bet you don't have any accounts on the social media he was using. The kids have a whole different set of apps they use."

Brunelle twisted his face into an exaggerated frown. "What's an app?" he demanded grumpily.

Carlisle looked again to Chen. "Please hurry, before Dave starts posting about the kids next door coming onto his lawn."

Chen took his leave and Carlisle was left standing in Brunelle's doorway. He knew he was supposed to ask Carlisle if she wanted to go on a double date with him and Casey.

"Anything else?" Carlisle asked.

Brunelle hesitated, but only for a moment. "Nope."

CHAPTER 15

A few nights later found Brunelle downloading apps, creating accounts, and scrolling his phone in search of Caleb Hirsch's secret online journal. He didn't have high hopes that a man of his age would be able to successfully navigate the latest form of communication for people a generation (or two) younger than him, but Casey was over again and offered to help. Together they could both fail to find Caleb's online child-killing manifesto. Although that might be a good thing.

"Did you really make your user name 'David_Brunelle_17'?" Casey asked as she sat down next to him on the couch and handed him an after-dinner cocktail. The photograph of the skyline was still on the wall behind them. "Not very stealthy."

Brunelle frowned. "It's what they suggested. What should I have done?"

"Something cool and justice-y." Casey thought for a moment. "What about Justicon?"

"Justicon?" Brunelle laughed. "That sounds like some sort of robot vigilante."

"Exactly," Casey laughed. "JusticonPrime. Even better. What do you think?"

"I think it makes 'David_Brunelle_17' sound pretty good," he answered.

She pointed at his phone. "Use it for the next app."

"How do you know I won't find it on this app?" he asked.

She squinted at the phone, then nodded to herself. "Because no one under forty uses that app. That's for posting staged pictures of your kids and pretending like you're still connected to your high school friends."

"I don't have any kids," Brunelle pointed out.

"I'm aware," Casey replied. "And I'm fine with that. But the kids aren't on this."

"What are they on?"

Casey took Brunelle's phone and navigated to the app store. She found what she was looking for and clicked 'GET'. "This, JusticonPrime."

"I'm not using that name," Brunelle insisted.

Casey didn't say anything for a few moments. Her fingers danced across Brunelle's phone and then she handed it back to him. "Yes, you are. You're welcome."

Brunelle looked at his new account and username and sighed. "You think Caleb posted on this?"

"If he really was losing it, he might have started posting," Casey answered. "Not only would you see what he was saying, this one will be short videos of him saying it. You'll be able to judge his mental state for yourself."

"And so will the jury," Brunelle realized.

"Like I said," Casey kissed him on the cheek, "you're welcome."

Brunelle frowned for a moment, but then answered,

"Thank you."

Casey smiled at him, then disappeared into the kitchen for a while. Brunelle wasn't sure how long she was in there because he got sucked into the rabbit hole of his new app. What started as a search for users with names like 'Caleb_Hirsh_17' quickly devolved into a seemingly never-ending series of shortform videos. Everything from practical jokes, to dance moves, to minimalist ruminations on the brevity and futility of life.

At some point, Casey came out and stood in front of him, staring appraisingly at the wall above the couch.

"Maybe we should get something new for that wall," she said. "Not mine. Not yours. Ours."

"Mm-hm," Brunelle grunted without looking up.

Casey said something further about their shared décor or whatever, but he managed to ignore it as he surfed the functions of the app. The algorithm was learning his likes and dislikes and it was becoming increasingly difficult to turn away from the next suggested video and stay focused on his task of finding Caleb's account.

"Are you even listening to me?" he finally noticed Casey ask him, arms crossed and toe tapping.

"Um…" he started. "No. No, I am not."

Casey rolled her eyes and laughed. "Well, at least you're honest."

"I've been called worse," Brunelle replied.

"I said," Casey repeated herself, "have you talked to Gwen about going out on that double date?"

Brunelle thought for a moment. "You like it when I'm honest, right?"

"I expect you to be honest," Casey replied.

"Right," Brunelle said. "I have not asked her about it. It

hasn't really come up."

"I wouldn't think a double date would come up while you're talking about a murder case," Casey said. "You need to bring it up."

"Um, okay," Brunelle agreed in a way that strongly suggested disagreement. "It's just that..."

"Are you embarrassed by me?" Casey demanded.

Oh, fuck.

Brunelle set his phone down and gave his girlfriend his undivided attention. "Absolutely not."

Casey frowned. "You say that, but you don't act like it."

"What are you talking about?" Brunelle stood up. "Is this because I was focused on my phone just now? I'm sorry. I just got caught up. It's this case."

"It's not the case." Casey shook her head. "It's you. Or maybe it's me."

"It's not you," Brunelle insisted. He stepped forward and put a hand on his girlfriend's shoulder. "It's me. It's definitely me."

Casey frowned at him. But she didn't shrug his hand away. "I've been trying to ignore it. To give you your space or whatever. But it doesn't feel very good to have to beg someone to be with me. If you don't want to move in together, then just say so. I told you I expect you to be honest. I deserve that at least."

Brunelle knew she was right. "Okay. That's fair."

"I know it's fair," Casey snapped. She went ahead and pulled away from his hand. "I don't need you to tell me that. I need you to tell me what the hell is going on with you. And if you can't do that, maybe we need to reconsider."

"Reconsider what?" Brunelle asked. "Moving in together?"

"Everything, Dave," Casey answered. "Not just moving in together. Everything."

The words hit Brunelle like a blast of heat from a furnace. He recognized both the danger and the opportunity she was offering him. If he wanted out, she was pointing to the exit.

But he didn't want to leave. That was the entire point.

"I'm afraid," he said. "You want me to be honest? Fine. I'll be honest. I'm afraid."

Casey scowled at him. "What are you afraid of?"

"I'm afraid of screwing this up," Brunelle said. "I'm afraid of changing. I've screwed up more than my share of relationships. But this, what we have, it's..." he sought for the right word. "It's comfortable. In a good way. And I'm afraid if we change anything, it'll ruin everything."

Casey's expression softened slightly. "That's silly, Dave. You don't need to be afraid of us changing. We're supposed to change."

"But everything is good now," Brunelle protested. "It's comfortable and easy and effortless. It's like we're on autopilot."

"Autopilot is for planes, Dave, not relationships," Casey said. "Relationships are living, organic things. They will grow, one direction or another, whether you want them to or not. The trick is to do things that make them grow in a positive direction, because if you don't do that, they'll grow the other way, the wrong way. There's no autopilot for relationships. If you stay on autopilot too long you either crash into a mountain or you run out of fuel."

Brunelle had crashed into his share of mountains. Running out of fuel almost seemed serene. He didn't know what to say.

Casey put her hands on his shoulders and looked into his

eyes. "Do you trust me?"

He did.

"Yes."

"You don't want autopilot," she said. "You want a steering wheel and a stick shift on the floor. You want sharp turns and steep hills and rickety old bridges that might fall right out from under you. And you know what else you want?"

Brunelle held her deep, beautiful gaze. "What?"

"You want somebody in the passenger seat, screaming and laughing and living it all with you," she said. "I want you in my passenger seat. So, you need to figure it out: do you want me in your passenger seat?"

Brunelle nodded. He liked autopilot. But he liked Casey more.

"Yes," he told her, "I want you in my passenger seat."

Casey pulled him in for the tightest hug he'd ever gotten.

"But," he finally told her, "I don't want that fucking landscape over my couch."

CHAPTER 16

Brunelle wasn't able to find Caleb Hirsch's social media accounts from the outside. But Chen was able to find them from the inside. Subpoenas to several different tech companies for any and all accounts connected to Caleb's phone number or email address revealed numerous accounts. There were a few he had clearly abandoned. Older accounts on apps only old people like Brunelle were still using. Those were of no value. The one that did have value was his most recent one. The one JusticonPrime had failed to find after the agreement not to hang the landscape over his couch.

Chen had moved quickly to get the information the day before the hearing on Edwards's motion to dismiss. Brunelle, Carlisle, and Chen all assembled again in Brunelle's office and Chen fired up his laptop.

"You are not going to believe this stuff," Chen prefaced. "This guy had definitely lost it."

"Lost it, like his girlfriend was justified in killing him?" Brunelle questioned.

Chen declined to offer his opinion on the matter. "See for

yourself."

Chen cued up the first video and they all watched as Caleb Hirsch's face popped up in the frame. It was always strange to see someone alive after meeting them for the first time when they were dead.

'Hey there everybody. My name's Caleb and this is my first post. Uh, I don't really have much to say. Well, I mean I do, but I'm not gonna say it, you know? Not right now. But soon. Maybe. I hope. It just kinda depends. On like a lot of different stuff. Uh, yeah. So anyway. Yeah. Okay. Bye.'

Caleb appeared to be in his bedroom, although it was hard to tell because his face was so close to the camera barely any of the room behind him was visible. He seemed lucid enough, although Brunelle wasn't entirely sure what the yardstick was for that on social media.

"That seemed pretty benign," Brunelle remarked. "No real indications of homicidal ideation."

"So far, so good," Carlisle added.

But Chen withheld judgment. Or at least comment. "There's more." He cued up the next clip.

'Uh, hey, it's Caleb again. I know I don't really have any followers yet, but, you know, soon, right? In the meantime, uh, I just want to say that I know what's going on, okay? Like, I can see it. You might think I don't know, but I know. I know, man, and it's not cool. But there are more of us than them and so, like, if you understand what I'm saying, please follow me because I'm gonna have a lot more to say real soon. They think they can stop me but they can't stop me. No one can stop me from telling the truth. All right, Caleb out.'

Brunelle frowned. "That was a little more ominous," he allowed.

"Although his only threat was to tell the truth," Carlisle

noted. "You can't kill somebody for telling the truth."

Brunelle suspected that might be the motive in a lot of killings.

Carlisle saw his expression and added, "Not legally anyway."

Brunelle could agree with that.

"Next one," Chen said and started another clip.

Caleb was noticeably more agitated. He had dark bags under his eyes and he was even closer to the camera, filling the entire screen with his face.

'I know what you're doing. I know what you're doing, man, but it's not gonna work. I know why no one is following me, but I'm going to get the word out. I'm going to tell people. People are going to learn the truth and then you'll be exposed and then you won't be able to trick everyone anymore and you'll have to leave me alone. That's all I want, man. Just leave me alone. Leave me alone.'

Brunelle rubbed a hand across his chin. "This is really more sad than anything else. How many of these are there?"

"He started about thirty days before the murder," Chen explained. "There are one hundred and twelve of these."

"A hundred and twelve?" Brunelle leaned back and looked at the ceiling. "Are they all like this? Just pointless and cryptic?"

"Most of them," Chen admitted. "They get more relevant at the end."

"That makes sense," Carlisle said. "Maybe we should skip ahead to those. We can always go back through them all later. It might even help give us some context if we know what he said in the last ones."

Brunelle was hardly going to disagree. He didn't want to sit through another one hundred and nine clips of looking up

Caleb's nose while he babbled about shadow conspiracies.

"Let's start about five days out from the murder," Chen suggested. "That's when he starts talking about the school kids."

"Shit," Brunelle hissed. "So he did mention school kids."

Chen frowned and nodded. "Yeah."

"That's probably not good," Carlisle suspected.

"Probably not," Chen agreed. "But I think it's more nuanced than Zoey made it seem."

Brunelle supposed that could be true. But he braced himself for the worst, nonetheless.

Somewhat to Brunelle's surprise, Caleb looked a lot better in the next clip. More like the dead man he'd first seen on the porch, as strange as that might seem. There was a calmness in both versions that had been missing from the last video they had just watched.

'Hey there, everyone. Caleb here again. First of all, I just want to say thank you to everyone who's following this account. I know it can be a little uneven at times, so I appreciate you sticking it out. Things have been better lately. I've been working really hard and doing my best to take care of myself. It's not always easy, but it's always worth it. I just want to say that some of the things I've posted here, well, they're just not right. I mean, I believed them when I said them, but now, looking back... Well, part of healing is changing, and part of changing is moving on, and part of moving on is owning up to your mistakes. I'm not any different from anyone else. I've made mistakes, but I'm owning up and I'm changing and I'm healing. God bless.'

"That was awesome," Carlisle beamed. "Let's just play that in our opening statement, then point at Addison and say, 'And then she shot him'."

Chen raised a cautionary hand. "We're not done yet."

"Damn," Brunelle said.

"Yup," Chen agreed.

The next three clips were very similar. Caleb looked good, sounded calm, and didn't threaten the mass murder of children. Then they reached the last video.

"He did this one two days before he was murdered," Chen set it up.

Caleb's face flashed onto the screen, but it wasn't the same face they had seen in the previous several videos. Not really. Not the eyes. They were wide, red-rimmed, wild.

'Okay, okay, okay. Tomorrow is the day, or maybe the day after. They think I don't know, but I know. I can't even sleep. I think I fooled them. I'm pretty sure I fooled them. Yeah, yeah, I fooled them. And now I'll show them. I'll show them they can't trick me. I'll show them all. They'll be sorry. They'll all be sorry.'

And the clip ended. Brunelle pursed his lips.

"That could have been worse," Carlisle said.

"It could have been better," Chen countered.

"It's what it is," Brunelle said. "It's not definitive. That will have to be good enough."

"Do you think he was talking about the kids?" Carlisle asked. "Do you think maybe Zoey was telling the truth?"

Brunelle didn't think that. Not yet. But he was finding it harder to maintain his opinion.

"She wasn't telling the whole truth," Chen answered. "She wasn't completely lying either. I've been doing this a long time. I can tell when someone is being honest and I can tell when they're lying. And I can tell when they're holding something back. She was holding something back."

"What?" Brunelle asked. That was the key to the case.

But Chen could only shake his head. "I don't know."

CHAPTER 17

Chen didn't know. Which meant Edwards could fill it in with whatever she wanted. But not yet. That was for the trial. That would require Zoey Addison to take the stand. That would open her up to cross-examination. That would give Brunelle a chance to show the jury she was lying. That she didn't have to kill Caleb Hirsch. That she was a murderer.

But first came Edwards's motion to dismiss. At that hearing, there was no evidence from the defense. No testimony from the defendant. No filling in the holes in the State's case. Edwards was asserting the State's case, as it was, was insufficient as a matter of law. It was based on all of the evidence collected to date.

Unfortunately, Brunelle had more evidence for her.

He dropped a pair of CDs onto the file she was reviewing in the courtroom immediately prior to the hearing.

"What are these?" She looked up from her now-blocked notes.

"CDs," Brunelle answered.

"We can give you a thumb drive," Carlisle offered, "if that's easier."

It was 8:45 a.m., fifteen minutes before the hearing. The hearing had been assigned to Judge Michael Gonzalez. Edwards had gotten to the courtroom first and staked out her position at the defense table. Brunelle and Carlisle were next to arrive, setting their own materials on the prosecution table before confronting Edwards. Zoey Addison would arrive soon from the jail, escorted by two corrections officers, who would spend the hearing seated within lunging distance of her and trying not to look as excruciatingly bored as they were. The last to appear would be the court staff. First the bailiff and court reporter, then finally, when everyone was properly assembled, the judge.

"A thumb drive would be nice," Edwards accepted Carlisle's offer. "My laptop doesn't even have a slot for CDs. Those are pretty ten years ago, Dave."

Brunelle didn't feel like arguing. Carlisle didn't come to his defense either.

"But what's on these?" Edwards repeated her inquiry. "Are you really dumping new evidence on me ten minutes before my motion to dismiss for insufficient evidence?"

"Twelve minutes," Brunelle corrected, "and yes we are doing exactly that. Sorry."

Edwards closed her eyes and pinched the bridge of her nose. "Why didn't I get these sooner, whatever they are? Wait, it's not the journal, is it?"

"It is not the journal," Brunelle answered.

But Carlisle disagreed. "It's kind of his journal. It's his social media posts leading up to his murder."

"His death," Edwards argued. "It's only murder if it's illegal, and it's not illegal if she acted out of necessity."

"It was murder," Brunelle insisted.

"Agree to disagree," Edwards replied. "And let the judge decide." She looked at the CDs. "So, who do these help? Me or you? You're giving them to me, so I assume they help you."

"We're giving them to you because we have to give you everything whether it helps us or not," Brunelle reminded her.

"How ethical of you," Edwards remarked. "But you still haven't answered my question. Who does this help? Does it have something that shows Zoey was lying about those school kids across the street?"

Brunelle frowned, with a quick glance at Carlisle and then back to Edwards. "No," he admitted. "No, it does not."

Their conversation was interrupted by the clank of the jail guards opening the secure side door to the courtroom. In marched Zoey Addison, flanked by two corrections officers. She wore the same red jail scrubs Brunelle had seen her in at the arraignment. Her expression was mostly numb. It was likely she didn't understand the arguments Edwards was planning to make to the judge. It was certain she wouldn't understand how Brunelle had just thrown a monkey wrench into those plans.

"I'm going to need a minute to explain," she gestured at the CDs, "all of this to my client."

"Of course," Brunelle answered. He looked at the clock on the wall. The judge would be out in four minutes. He and Carlisle retreated to the prosecution table as Edwards turned to her newly seated client and began whispering in her ear.

"What do you suppose she's saying?" Carlisle wondered aloud.

"Something terrible about us, I'm sure," Brunelle answered, "and their options on how to proceed this morning."

The bailiff and court reporter entered the courtroom next,

wordlessly taking up their positions in what was called 'the lower bench', that area directly beneath the judge. Edwards was running out of time.

A minute later, Judge Gonzalez entered to the call of the bailiff: "All rise! The King County Superior Court is in session, The Honorable Michael Gonzalez presiding!"

Gonzalez was a perfectly adequate judge for the hearing. Not known as being either particularly prosecution-friendly or defense-friendly, he had mostly done family law before running for judge and winning an open seat vacated by a retirement from the previous generation of judges. He'd been on the bench long enough to have gained a considerable amount of experience presiding over criminal cases. He was unlikely to dismiss a murder case for insufficiency of the evidence. But he was very likely to disapprove of Brunelle dumping discovery on Edwards literally minutes before the hearing he had cleared his schedule to preside over.

Everyone stood up and Brunelle stole a glance over at the defense table. Addison looked stunned. Edwards looked angry. That was probably about right.

"Are the parties ready," Judge Gonzalez asked, "on the matter of *The State of Washington versus Zoey Addison?*"

The question was usually just a formality. A way of saying 'Good morning' to the litigants who had assembled in his courtroom. Not that morning.

"No, Your Honor," Edwards practically spat. "The defense is not ready."

Gonzalez raised a surprised eyebrow at Edwards's announcement.

"The defense is not ready," she continued, "because the State just dumped brand new evidence on us." She held up the

CDs for the judge. "And I don't even know what the evidence is because I'm going to have to go back to my office to even view whatever it is that's on these."

Judge Gonzalez frowned, then turned to the prosecution. "Is that true, counsel?"

Carlisle looked to Brunelle to reply. He was lead counsel after all. He sighed.

"Yes, Your Honor," he admitted. "We did provide new discovery to the defense this morning, but we only received it ourselves yesterday."

"Getting it yesterday would have been better than today," Edwards grumbled.

"It takes time to review, copy, and disseminate discovery," Brunelle explained. "This morning was the soonest we could reasonably provide it, and we made sure to do so before the case was called for the hearing."

"By four minutes, Your Honor," Edwards snapped. "Four minutes."

"All right, all right." Judge Gonzalez held his hands up. "I'm not one to stand on ceremony, but this will degenerate quickly if I allow you to argue at each other instead of addressing your comments to the bench."

Brunelle agreed, not least because he didn't want Edwards to keep yelling at him.

"Given that this is a motion regarding the sufficiency of the State's evidence," Gonzalez understood, "I imagine this new information could impact the arguments. Would you agree, Ms. Edwards?"

She could hardly disagree, but she wasn't about to concede either. "Not if you suppress the evidence, Your Honor. It was provided late. The remedy for late discovery is suppression. Suppress it and then let's proceed on the evidence provided up and until 8:55 this morning."

Brunelle shook his head. "Suppression is only a remedy if the discovery is so late that it impacts the trial, not a pretrial hearing. This isn't a situation where we dumped new evidence on the defense on the eve of trial. We are weeks away from trial. This motion can be rescheduled. It's inconvenient, but it would be completely inappropriate to exclude relevant evidence from a murder trial just because it was discovered shortly before a discretionary motion the defense attorney decided to schedule on a random date weeks before the case goes in front of a jury."

"I'm allowed to bring motions prior to the trial, Your Honor," Edwards called out. "In fact, I have an ethical duty to do so. My client is charged with murder for stopping someone else from committing even more murders. The law recognizes that is not a crime. The defense of necessity is well-established in the case law. But despite her obvious innocence, she is sitting in jail, awaiting her trial where any reasonable jury will acquit her of the charge. Of course I scheduled this motion in advance of the trial. Every day she sits in jail is a miscarriage of justice and I have an obligation to my client and to the criminal justice system as a whole to bring an end to injustice as quickly as I can. I shouldn't be penalized for that and neither should my client."

"Her job is to get killers acquitted," Carlisle whispered to Brunelle. "That's actually injustice. Just sayin'."

Carlisle had a point. So did Edwards. But the truth was, sometimes things just don't go the way everyone might like. Brunelle told the judge as much in his reply.

"This is not how I would have wanted discovery to have proceeded in this case, Your Honor," he offered, "but this is how it happened and it's what we have to deal with. Ms. Addison shot and killed her boyfriend, Caleb Hirsch. No one contests that. Ms. Edwards says her client is a hero because Mr. Hirsch was about to go on a murderous rampage. The CDs we provided this morning contain shortform video clips Mr. Hirsch made in the weeks leading up to his death, and his alleged plot to murder school children. I'm a little surprised Ms. Edwards is making a motion to suppress those videos without even having looked at them. What if they amount to a confession of his intentions and a vindication of Ms. Addison's actions? We could take advantage of that and agree to suppressing the best evidence her client could possibly ask for. But we are not doing that. We are simply providing evidence as fast as we could after we received it and asking the Court to hear and rule on Ms. Edwards's motion to dismiss—but later."

Another stolen glance revealed Edwards's expression had turned again. She was still angry, but she also knew Brunelle had a point. More importantly, so did the judge.

"Are you sure you wouldn't prefer to review this new evidence," he asked, "before moving to suppress it, Ms. Edwards?"

"Fuck," Brunelle heard Edwards hiss under her breath. She threw her arms up. "Fine. Yes. Yes, Your Honor. I need to review this new evidence. I'm sure it's not the exculpatory silver bullet Mr. Brunelle teases it might be. In fact, if it were, he would be ethically obligated to dismiss the case without me even having to review it. But he hasn't done that, has he? So, fine, I will ask the Court to set this hearing over one week to allow me to review this new evidence. I would also ask leave to amend my briefing as may be required by this new information."

"No objection to either of those suggestions, Your Honor," Brunelle was quick to agree. "We will be prepared in one week to argue that the evidence, these CDs included, is more than sufficient to allow the case to go to a jury."

Judge Gonzalez was obviously irritated by the small circus he had just been made to preside over. But, as Brunelle said, sometimes things don't go according to plan. Maybe even most of the time.

"The matter will be rescheduled to one week from today," Gonzalez ruled. "The defense may supplement its briefing based on the new evidence. The State may not. Be prepared to argue the motion on its merits when we reconvene. I will not delay the hearing any further."

Small wins were still wins. Brunelle wanted to apologize to Edwards again, off the record, but she was already deep into a huddled conversation with her client even as the guards circled their table, eager to get Addison back to her cell.

"We should probably go," he suggested to Carlisle, picking up his file.

"'Ya think?" She started for the exit. "Now's our chance. I wouldn't turn your back on Jess until she calms down a bit. Maybe she'll like what's on those videos enough to realize we did her a favor."

Brunelle saw the opening. It was small and he didn't want to take it. But he knew he'd have to answer for it if he didn't.

"Speaking of favors..." he said as they walked into the courthouse hallway.

Carlisle stopped in her tracks and frowned at him. "I already don't like the sound of that."

"I barely said anything," Brunelle defended.

"You said enough." Carlisle narrowed her eyes at him. "If it was about the case, you would have just told me what you needed me to do. A task isn't a favor. A favor is," she sneered slightly at the thought, "personal."

"We can't have a personal relationship too?" Brunelle deflected.

"It depends," Carlisle answered. "What's this favor?"

Brunelle sighed. There was no point to beating any more around the bush. "Casey saw your new haircut and new clothes and thinks you have a new girlfriend. She wants to go out on a double date."

Carlisle just stared at Brunelle for several very long, very awkward seconds. Finally, she crossed her arms and narrowed her eyes at him. "Where?"

"What?"

"Where?" she repeated. "Where would this double date be?"

Brunelle hadn't expected that reaction. "Um, like a restaurant, I think. I'm not completely sure."

"GlasHaus," Carlisle said.

Brunelle took a beat. "What?"

"GlasHaus," Carlisle repeated. "It's a restaurant."

"I know it's a restaurant," Brunelle said. "It's like the fanciest restaurant in the city. I was thinking maybe someplace more like—"

"I'll go if it's GlasHaus," Carlisle interrupted. "Abby wants to go to GlasHaus but I can't stand the idea of sitting in a fancy restaurant for two hours trying to think of conversation. Fancy is not my thing and small talk is not my thing. With you two there, I get credit for taking her to GlasHaus, and you can do the small talk for me."

Brunelle cocked his head at his partner. "This kind of feels like plea bargaining."

Carlisle nodded. "Sure. We each have a client. Yours

wants to double date and mine wants to go to GlasHaus. Win-win."

Brunelle thought for a moment. Carlisle was right. He stuck out his hand. "Deal."

CHAPTER 18

Casey was almost ready. She was leaning forward, looking into the bathroom mirror, putting on her earrings. Brunelle was sitting on the bed, hands between his knees. He had finished getting ready first, but then again, he didn't have to worry about things like earrings.

"I'm kind of surprised Gwen agreed to this so easily," Casey called from the bathroom. "I was half joking when I told you to ask."

Brunelle nodded. "I was surprised too. But apparently we're helping her impress this Abby, so she's getting a benefit out of it. A quid pro quo. I'm not sure she would have agreed otherwise."

"Do you know Abby?" Casey asked, emerging from the bathroom, fully earringed and ready for a night at Seattle's fanciest restaurant.

"No." Brunelle stood up and took a look at his girlfriend. "But if she's half as beautiful as you, Gwen is a lucky woman."

Casey smacked him on the chest. "Flatterer." But her smile was genuine and warm.

They walked into the living room to grab their coats and head out.

"Now, we need to have three topics of conversation ready, in case things start to get awkward," Casey said.

"Preplanned conversation topics?" Brunelle questioned. "That seems kind of fake."

"It's smart," Casey replied. "The only thing you and Carlisle have in common is your work and I don't think Abby, whoever she is, will want to spend two hours talking about murders."

Brunelle supposed that might be true. "So, what? Like the weather? Sports?"

Casey put a fist on her hips and looked disapprovingly at him. "Sports?"

"Sure." Brunelle shrugged. "Everybody loves the Seahawks. Everybody misses the Sonics. Everybody just kind of feels bad for the Mariners."

"What about the Kraken?" Casey asked.

Brunelle pointed at his girlfriend. "Yes, we can talk about the Kraken."

Casey pointed back. "No. No Kraken. No Seahawks. No Mariners."

"Sonics?" Brunelle tried.

"No Sonics, no Storm, no Sounders."

Brunelle frowned. Casey handed him his coat from the front closet.

"I mean, if it turns out she's a huge sports fan, then great, knock yourself out," Casey said as she pulled her own coat on, "but we can't rely on that. These need to be things about Abby, so she gets a chance to talk about herself. Everybody likes talking about themselves. It'll help her open up a bit."

"So, what do you do for a living? Where were you born? Stuff like that?"

Casey shook her head. "No, no. That's a job interview. This is dinner. One topic that always works is to ask her if she's gone on any interesting trips lately."

"Oh, okay," Brunelle answered. "That makes sense. And maybe ask her if she has any trips planned."

Casey shook her head as she opened the door to the hallway. "No. See, you have to ask about past trips. Asking about future trips automatically raises the question about whether she would take those trips with Gwen. Talking about future stuff together is way too much pressure on a new relationship."

Brunelle had to laugh. "Too much pressure? Like deciding to move in together? What about organic relationship growing or whatever?"

Casey laughed back, warmly, a bit to Brunelle's surprise. He half-expected a scolding glare. But she smiled and grabbed his hand as the door closed behind them and they headed for the elevators.

"That reminds me," she said. "We might want to rethink moving into your condo. My house is bigger." She squeezed his hand without looking at him. "And I'm late."

CHAPTER 19

GlasHaus was everything Brunelle had expected. The décor was impeccable, with just the right mix of classic leathers and fabrics with contemporary art and extras, all bathed in the perfect level of dimmed lighting and background music. One entire wall was floor-to-ceiling windows with breathtaking views of Lake Union and the Seattle skyline beyond, visible from every table in the restaurant. And the food — the food was honestly the best food Brunelle had ever eaten. He didn't even understand how the cook could pull those flavors from what he had ordered. Even the conversation was vibrant and spritely, despite their concerns. No need to ask preplanned questions about recent holidays or sportsball teams. And Brunelle could barely enjoy any of it.

'I'm late.'

"Are you sure?" he had asked, stupidly.

"Am I sure I'm late?" Casey had replied. "Yes, I know my own body, thank you."

"I mean, are you sure you're pregnant?"

"I am very much not sure I'm pregnant," Casey had

answered. "That's why I said, 'I'm late' and not, 'I'm pregnant'."

"Should we pick up a test?" Brunelle had suggested. "On the way to the restaurant?"

Casey had laughed. "No. I am not peeing on a stick at GlasHaus. We can pick it up on the way home. Nothing is going to change between now and the end of the evening."

And so there they sat, at a table one row from the actual window, seated so Gwen and Abby had the best view, and Brunelle doing his level best not to wish the night away.

As it turned out, Abby was more than interested in their latest case. She didn't work at the courthouse as Casey had guessed. Rather, she was a pediatrician who worked at a clinic about three blocks north on 4th Avenue. A new coffee shop opened up about halfway between her office and the courthouse and she and Carlisle had happened to try it out for the first time on the same day. They had ordered the exact same drink, so when the barista called out the order, they both reached for the same cup. And the rest was history. Or at least a few weeks anyway. It was probably too soon to know whether it would be history worth remembering, but right then, they seemed to like each other very much.

Abby was in her mid-30s, like Carlisle, and seemed to share a similar edge, at least in her sense of humor. She had wavy brown hair cut short enough to bounce when she turned her head, and wore a lovely evening dress for the date to GlasHaus that Carlisle had finally managed to schedule. Even if it was with two strangers. But she didn't seem to mind at all.

"So, explain this whole 'necessity' defense to me again." She leaned forward, her last bite of chicken impaled on her fork. "It's okay to murder people if they're going to murder more people?"

"It's a little more limited than that," Carlisle said.

"Yeah, there's a specific test that has to be met," Brunelle added, "and the defendant has to prove it at trial. There's like four elements of the defense."

"One, the defendant was seeking to prevent some bad thing from happening," Carlisle listed the first element.

"The bad thing the defendant was trying to prevent," Brunelle reported the second and third element, "has to be worse than the bad thing the defendant does to prevent it. And it can't be the defendant's fault that the bad thing has to be prevented."

"And the last part," Casey, the detective, knew, "is that there was no other legal alternative available. You can't shoot him if you could have called 911 instead."

Abby frowned. "Can 911 respond that fast?"

Casey shook her head. "No," she admitted. "That's why it was probably necessity."

"Maybe necessity," Brunelle challenged. "It's only necessity if she was telling the truth when she said he was going to go to the school. For all we know, he was leaving her and she made up the whole school kid thing after the fact to try to get out of it."

"Ugh, and children too." Abby shook her head. "I love kids. That's why I went into pediatrics." She looked at Brunelle and Casey. "Do you two have kids?"

Brunelle froze for a moment. "Uh..." He turned to Casey. "No? No, right?"

"Er, right," Casey stammered. "No kids."

Brunelle looked back to Abby. "Nope. No kids."

Carlisle frowned at them. "That was weird."

Abby didn't notice. "Did the guy ever tell anyone he was going to murder school kids?" she asked. "I mean anyone besides his girlfriend who obviously could be lying."

Carlisle pursed her lips. "He sort of suggested it to his psychiatrist, but he didn't quite say it. The psychiatrist put something in his notes about it maybe being in the guy's journal, but we never found a journal. We did find a bunch of online videoclips he did where he was saying some weird shit, but he never explicitly mentioned school kids. We figure those online clips were probably what the doc meant when he said 'journal'."

"Oh no, there's definitely a journal," Abby disagreed. "A real, physical journal. Doctors don't use metaphors in their chart notes. That would be ridiculous."

"Shit," Carlisle hissed. "That's what I was thinking too, but—"

"But if we don't find it," Brunelle finished the thought, "that's yet another motion to dismiss Edwards will file."

"Why would she file a motion to dismiss?" Abby asked. "It's not your fault the journal is missing."

"She'll say it is," Carlisle explained. "The State has an obligation to protect and preserve evidence. Even exculpatory evidence."

"Especially exculpatory evidence," Casey put in.

Brunelle nodded. "Especially exculpatory evidence," he agreed.

"But if you never had it, how can you preserve it?" Abby asked.

"Well, see, you're thinking like a rational person," Brunelle said, "but this is a motion by a defense attorney."

"Are defense attorneys not rational?" Abby questioned.

"Of course they are," Brunelle allowed.

"And Edwards isn't just rational," Carlisle said. "She's smart."

"You have to remember that there's a system already in place," Brunelle explained, "and the entire system is intentionally slanted in favor of the defendant. A defendant is presumed innocent. The State has to prove each element of the charge beyond a reasonable doubt. We have to share every last piece of evidence with the defense, well in advance of trial, but they don't have to tell us anything until right before they use it, if they use it at all."

"A defense attorney is ethically bound to seek the best possible result for their client," Carlisle expounded, "even if that means securing an acquittal for a defendant they know is guilty."

"But we can't seek a conviction of a defendant we know is innocent," Brunelle continued. "That would be completely unethical."

"And terrifying," Abby said. "Knowingly putting an innocent person in prison?"

"Exactly," Casey said. "So, the cops are supposed to find all of the evidence, even the evidence that helps the defendant."

"Oh, okay. The defense attorney will claim you didn't collect the journal because it would have helped the defendant." Abby was starting to understand. "And if you really did that, then you would be trying to put an innocent person in prison."

"Exactly," Carlisle confirmed.

Abby shook her head. "You better find that journal."

Brunelle already knew that. Carlisle did too.

Then Abby asked the most important question. "What if you do find it, and what if it says exactly what the defendant told you? What if it says, 'Tomorrow morning I'm going to go across the street and murder dozens of school children and the only way anyone can stop me is if my girlfriend shoots me on my way out the door'?"

Brunelle and Carlisle just looked at each other and frowned.

"The right thing to do would be to dismiss the case," Casey answered for them.

"Can you do that?" Abby asked. "Does the prosecutor have the power to just dismiss the case?"

Brunelle nodded. "Yeah, we do. And if it really is the right thing to do, we have to."

Abby reached over and grabbed Carlisle's hand. "Promise me you'll do the right thing, Gwen. I need to know you're the kind of person who would do the right thing."

Carlisle smiled slightly. "Of course I'll do the right thing," she said. What else could she say in that moment?

Casey only needed to look at Brunelle for him to know he had to answer the question too. "Yes, we'll do the right thing," he promised. "But this is all academic because we're never going to find the journal, and if we do, it's not going to say that." It was time to change the subject. "Now, let's talk about doing the wrong thing. Who wants dessert?"

                              * * *

The double date had been a tremendous success. Good food, good company, good conversation. And excellent desserts.

The four of them exited the restaurant to say their goodbyes out under the stars. Brunelle and Casey had parked in the restaurant's lot. Carlisle and Abby had parked on the street about a block away.

After a round of "It was nice to meet you", "That was fun", and "Let's do this again sometime", the foursome split into twosomes for the ride home. But before they could even take a step toward his car, Casey tugged on Brunelle's arm.

"Look!" She pointed across the busy four-lane arterial

street in front of the restaurant. "There's a drugstore across the street. We can pick up a pregnancy test before we drive home."

There was a marked crosswalk and the signal had just switched to 'WALK'. It should have been safe to cross. But paint and signs were only safe if everyone else on the road obeyed their own paint and signs too. That was why Driving Under the Influence was illegal.

Brunelle heard the engine before he saw the car. It crested the hill to their left and went airborne for a moment. When it landed, the driver lost control and swerved toward the shoulder. Toward the sidewalk. Toward Casey. The car careened back into the roadway, ignoring the marked crosswalk, Casey's 'WALK' sign, and its own red light.

Brunelle reached for Casey. But he was late too.

CHAPTER 20

Casey managed to turn just slightly as the front passenger fender clipped her across the legs. She went flying to the ground and cracked her head on the asphalt. The car smashed full force into a parked car on the other side of the intersection. Brunelle ran to where Casey landed, laying face up against the curb, unconscious. There was blood coming out of her nose and mouth.

Carlisle and Abby ran over too. They'd barely made it halfway to their car. Abby stuck her fingers against Casey's neck. "She has a pulse," she reported.

That was more than Brunelle hoped for the driver who was trapped in the twisted wreckage next to them. The car's horn was blaring and people all around were gasping and shrieking. Carlisle took out her phone but the sirens were already on their way.

Brunelle wanted to pick Casey up, at least cradle her head in his lap, but he knew he shouldn't move her, in case there were spinal injuries. All he could do was kneel next to her and think about all the cases he had where a person, after a single punch, had fallen backward onto the sidewalk, hitting the back of their head on the cement, and fracturing the delicate bone that rested under the brain. The brain would start bleeding and with no way for the blood to escape the brain cavity, it only took minutes for the pressure to crush the brain and kill the person. He placed his fingers gently on Casey's face and counted the impossibly infinite seconds until the ambulance arrived.

The next minutes were a blur of medical personnel and police officers. Casey was evaluated, then loaded into an ambulance. Brunelle was allowed to ride in the back with her. Carlisle and Abby stayed behind to talk to the cops. They would meet Brunelle at the hospital. Casey didn't regain consciousness on the trip. Brunelle held her hand and stared at the monitor displaying her heartbeat and oxygen levels. He wasn't a doctor but he allowed himself to hope.

The ride to Harborview Medical Center, Seattle's top trauma hospital, was relatively quick. Once there, Casey was loaded out and rushed through the emergency room into the examining rooms in the back. Brunelle was screened and asked to wait in the lobby. He wasn't legally family, and he would only get in the way anyway. He knew all of that, but it didn't make waiting any easier.

Neither did the arrival of Carlisle and Abby. Then Chen. He'd heard about the incident over dispatch. It was Vehicular Assault—Vehicular Homicide if the doctors didn't do their jobs. When Chen heard who the victim was, he made a call to determine the treating hospital and got confirmation when he was already halfway there.

"How is she?" he asked as he walked up to Brunelle.

Brunelle, seated in a waiting room chair and slouched forward with his head on his hands, just shrugged. "I don't know. She's been back there for almost an hour. They told me she's in serious condition."

"That's good actually," Abby said. "Critical means it's life-threatening. Serious means it's not."

"That's something," Carlisle suggested.

Brunelle supposed it was, but he wasn't feeling very lucky right then. Finally the door to the back opened and a nurse stepped out. "Mr. Brunelle?"

Brunelle popped to his feet. "Yes?"

"Casey is awake now," the nurse said, "if you'd like to come see her."

Brunelle didn't even answer or say goodbye to the others. He raced to the door and hurried down the maze of hallways to where the nurse indicated Casey was resting, if not exactly comfortably.

"Dave," she rasped with a tight grin as he entered. "I forgot to look both ways."

"No, that bastard was drunk and ran you down," Brunelle replied angrily. Then he surrendered his own weak smile. "How are you? What did the doctor say?"

"Broken femur," Casey reported. "Fractured ribs. Dislocated shoulder. Concussion. He said I was lucky I landed on my side. My shoulder took most of the fall before my head hit the pavement."

No internal skull fracture. Brunelle sighed with relief.

"Oh, and I'm not pregnant," Casey added with a hoarse chuckle.

"They checked if you were pregnant?" Brunelle questioned.

"Routine bloodwork for women of child-bearing age, they said," Casey explained. "So, we saved money on that home test."

Brunelle shook his head. "How can you make jokes with

what just happened?"

"How can I not?" Casey replied. She raised her hand weakly and Brunelle seized it. "This is a good reminder that none of us is guaranteed another day."

"I can remember that without you getting hit by a car," Brunelle complained.

The doctor appeared then, pulling back the curtain that separated Casey's bed from the rest of the room.

"Hi there!" he called out, far too chipper under the circumstances, in Brunelle's opinion. "I'm Dr. Yar. How's my favorite broken leg patient doing?"

He was young and happy and it made Brunelle feel old and unhappy.

"I'm good," Casey croaked. "A little thirsty."

"That's good," Yar replied. "It means you're alive. I'll have the nurse bring you some water." He looked to Brunelle. "Is this the husband?"

"Boyfriend," Casey corrected.

"We live together," Brunelle amended, if perhaps a bit prematurely.

"Nice," Yar remarked. "So, you have someone to help take care of you. That's going to be important. You're not going to be walking for a while."

"How long?" Brunelle asked. Not that he minded taking care of Casey, but he would need to make arrangements.

Yar shrugged slightly. "Most femoral fractures take about four to six months to fully heal."

Wow. Brunelle hadn't expected it to take that long.

"But you'll be able to get around on crutches before that," Yar continued. "It was a pretty clean break, so I don't anticipate any complications from the surgery."

"Surgery?" Brunelle questioned.

"Yes, most femur fractures require surgery," the doctor explained. "We need to make sure it sets properly. We'll put in some plates to help keep everything in proper position. Those will stay, so no second surgery and you get to set off the metal detectors at the airport now. Yay."

Brunelle didn't think that was a very substantial benefit.

The doctor seemed to sense Brunelle's disapproval. "Anyway, the femur is the strongest bone in your body. They support your weight and carry you everywhere. When one of them breaks, it takes a long time to be able to support your weight again." He pointed to Brunelle. "Good thing you'll have this guy around."

Casey grabbed Brunelle's hand again. "Yeah, good thing, huh?"

Brunelle squeezed Casey's hand. "A very good thing."

CHAPTER 21

Finally moving in together was indeed a good thing for Casey's convalescence, and for their relationship, but it was not such a great thing for Brunelle's job, or his commute. All of Casey's things were at her house in Bellevue and it just didn't make sense to try to move everything over to his place. Not at first anyway. So, instead of a quick trip to downtown from his Seattle condominium, Brunelle was forced to drive in from the suburbs, on the Interstate-90 floating bridge that spanned Lake Washington, along with everyone else who lived on the Eastside and worked downtown.

Working late also suddenly had a different significance. Before the accident, it meant little more than picking up takeout instead of cooking. After it, every minute Brunelle stayed late was a minute Casey had to struggle to get around her house on one good leg. She was never upset about it, but he felt guilty, nevertheless. And he had a trial approaching.

Thank God they didn't have kids.

The rescheduled hearing on Edwards's motion to dismiss for sufficiency of the evidence—or lack thereof—came just four days after the accident, three days after the surgery, and two days after Casey was discharged. By then, Brunelle was in no mood.

Edwards nodded to her opponents as Brunelle and Carlisle entered Judge Gonzalez's courtroom that morning. "Any last-minute evidence dumps today?" she asked, probably only half joking.

"No," was all Brunelle said, without even looking at her. He dropped his materials on the prosecution desk with a thud.

"Not your usual friendly self, I see," Carlisle commented as she, too, began to unpack her case file.

"I'm not getting a lot of rest lately," Brunelle explained. "Even with the drugs, Casey is in a lot of pain. She doesn't sleep well, so neither do I, especially when she needs to use the bathroom."

"That might be T.M.I.," Carlisle commented, "but I'll allow it since you guys are friends now."

Brunelle cocked her head at him. "Now?" he questioned.

"Vehicular assault notwithstanding, Abby really liked you guys," Carlisle said. "And I really like her. So, when Casey is up to it, we'd like to go out again. Maybe someplace really far away from any major roads, though."

Brunelle managed a half-smile. "Yeah, that would be nice."

The secure side door clanked open, and in walked Zoey Addison and her uniformed entourage. About a minute later, the bailiff and court reporter entered the courtroom, and a few seconds after that, Judge Gonzalez took the bench.

"All rise!" and all that, the bailiff called out.

The judge looked cautiously down at the litigants. "I ask this not just as a formality. Are the parties ready this time on the matter of *The State of Washington versus Zoey Addison*?"

"The State is ready, Your Honor," Brunelle answered for the prosecution.

"The defense is ready as well, Your Honor," Edwards confirmed.

Judge Gonzalez exhaled audibly. "Good. Is there anything we need to take up before we begin arguments?"

"Nothing from the State, Your Honor," Brunelle answered.

"And nothing from the defense," Edwards confirmed.

"All right then," the judge replied. "I will let you know that I have reread all of the briefing filed before the last hearing. I did not see any additional briefing from the defense. Is that correct, Ms. Edwards?"

"That's correct, Your Honor," Edwards answered. "There was nothing in those CDs that changes our argument. If anything, it strengthens it, and I will explain that in my comments to the Court."

"Thank you, Ms. Edwards," Judge Gonzalez responded. "This is the defense's motion, so I will hear first from Ms. Edwards. Whenever you're ready, counsel."

Edwards stood up to address the Court, straightened her suit, and took a deep breath. "The Court should dismiss this case because the State's evidence can and does lead to only one possible result. My client's actions meet the elements of the defense of necessity, and she is therefore not guilty of the crime of murder. No reasonable jury could find otherwise, and so it would be a waste of time and resources to allow the case to proceed to trial."

Brunelle frowned slightly. That was the headline. Now the argument would turn to the facts. His facts. The facts that, in his humble opinion, added up to murder.

"The facts in this case are generally agreed, Your Honor," Edwards continued. "Indeed, to bring this motion, we have to agree to the State's evidence and then explain why that evidence is insufficient as a matter of law to support the charges. Here, there is no dispute that my client shot her boyfriend, Caleb Hirsch. There is also no dispute that Mr. Hirsch died as a result of my client's actions."

Edwards pointed to the prosecution table. "The State would like the Court to stop there, but there is also no dispute that my client shot her boyfriend in order to prevent the far greater harm of Mr. Hirsch committing multiple other murders, and of innocent school children. That is what Ms. Addison told the police that very morning, while Mr. Hirsch's body was still blocking the front entrance of their home, and there is absolutely no evidence to the contrary. Accordingly, Your Honor, the State's uncontroverted evidence is that Ms. Addison shot and killed Mr. Hirsch and in so doing prevented him from murdering countless others. That is necessity."

Having summarized the relevant facts, Edwards took a moment before turning to the applicable law. She pulled out her copy of the criminal jury instructions and opened to the page marked with a pink sticky note.

"Necessity," Edwards read from the pattern instruction, "is a defense to a charge of murder if the following elements are met: one, the defendant reasonably believed the commission of the crime was necessary to avoid or minimize a harm; two, the harm sought to be avoided was greater than the harm resulting from a violation of the law; three, the threatened harm was not brought about by the defendant; and four, no reasonable legal alternative existed.

"In the case here," she continued, "Ms. Addison shooting

her boyfriend was necessary to stop him from going to the schoolyard and slaughtering children. The slaughtering of school children would have been far greater than the death of one person. It was in no way Ms. Addison's fault that Mr. Hirsch planned to do what he planned to do. And finally, there was no time for any other legal alternative. Mr. Hirsch was already in the doorway. The only other possible course of action would have been to call 911, but there is no way the police could have responded in the time it would have taken Mr. Hirsch to cross the street. Therefore, based on the State's own investigation and evidence, the defense of necessity has been met, and no reasonable jury could find otherwise. Thank You, Your Honor."

Judge Gonzalez nodded and turned to the prosecution table. "Who will be responding on behalf of the State?"

Brunelle stood up. "I will, Your Honor."

Gonzalez nodded again. "Whenever you're ready, Mr. Brunelle."

Oh, he was ready.

"The defense argument is laughable and their motion to dismiss is completely without merit." A bit strong, Brunelle knew, but he wasn't in the mood to worry about professional feelings. "Ms. Edwards read the jury instruction for necessity, but failed to include the last sentence." He didn't need to read from the book; he had it memorized. "'If you find that the *defendant* has established this defense, it will be your duty to return a verdict of not guilty.' The defendant, Your Honor. The defendant has to establish this."

He pointed at Edwards. "They have to put on evidence and tell the jury it was necessity, which presupposes that the State has already put on sufficient evidence in its case-in-chief to establish the crime. So, this entire motion is ridiculous. We will put on evidence that the defendant shot and killed the victim, then we will sit down. That's sufficient. If they then want to put on evidence of necessity, they have a right to do that, but at trial. The very trial they are trying to avoid with this premature, meritless motion to dismiss."

Judge Gonzalez frowned down from the bench. "Can't an affirmative defense be established by the State's own evidence? Is a defendant really required to put on evidence of necessity if the State's evidence already did so?"

"It won't in this case," Brunelle answered, avoiding the larger question.

"But what about the defendant's statement to police?" the judge inquired.

"We don't have to offer that, Your Honor," Brunelle responded. "In fact, why would we? Why would we have our detective turn to the jury and recite the defendant's hastily formed, untrue excuse? If the defense wants the jury to hear that the defendant really had no choice, they are going to have to put Ms. Addison on the stand and open her up to cross-examination about that claim. We won't be introducing her claims, and under the evidence rules, Ms. Edwards can't elicit her own client's statement through another witness. That's self-serving hearsay and is absolutely inadmissible."

Judge Gonzalez's frown turned thoughtful. He looked again to the defense. "What about that, Ms. Edwards? If the State elects not to introduce your client's statement, how could the jury find necessity without your client testifying, which would, by its nature, happen in front of the jury you're trying to avoid."

Edwards stood again. "Well, if the State is saying they don't intend to introduce any of my client's statements, then I would change my argument to say the Court should dismiss for lack of evidence because they can't prove Ms. Addison was the shooter. The only evidence of that was her confession."

Judge Gonzalez raised an eyebrow and turned back to the prosecution. "What about that Mr. Brunelle? Do you have evidence that Ms. Addison was the shooter other than her statements?"

"We will only introduce the part of her statement where she admits to shooting Mr. Hirsch," Brunelle answered.

"And we will then move to introduce the entirety of her statement," Edwards interjected, "under Evidence Rule 106, the Rule of Completeness."

"And we can have that argument in front of the trial judge, Your Honor," Brunelle said. "But to do that, this Court needs to deny the defendant's motion today to allow the case to proceed to that trial, and that judge, and that motion."

Gonzalez smirked. "Do you really think a judge would let you introduce only the first half of a murder confession? Just the part about doing it, but not the part about why? How would that be fair?"

"I don't know about fair, Your Honor," Brunelle returned, "but it complies with the evidence rules."

"I'm not sure," Carlisle whispered from her seat next to Brunelle, "you should tell the judge we don't care about fairness."

Judge Gonzalez seemed to agree with Carlisle's sentiment, even if he hadn't heard it.

"Isn't the prosecutor supposed to seek a just result, according to the law and the facts," the judge challenged, "not seek to win the case at any cost?"

Brunelle sighed. He didn't need to be lectured by a judge—someone who quit the game to become a referee—about what his ethical obligations were. But he didn't want to lose the hearing either.

"Of course, Your Honor," he answered. "But it has been my experience, after, lo, these many years as a prosecutor, that a defendant's claims to law enforcement are not always the most solid ground upon which to build a monument to justice."

"Poetic," Carlisle whispered, either admiringly or mockingly. Brunelle wasn't sure. It was probably both.

"But I think, Your Honor," Brunelle continued, "that we may be getting a bit too far into the weeds on this. Let's not overthink it and try to anticipate every possible evidentiary ruling of a trial court. In truth, the fact that we're doing that shows that the case can and should proceed to a trial. This motion is supposed to assume the truth of the State's evidence, and adopt any and all reasonable inferences from that evidence in favor of the State, and if you do that, is there any reasonable jury that could possibly find guilty a woman who shot her boyfriend six times in the back? Can this Court really say that's absolutely impossible? That no jury could possibly decide not to believe the defendant when she claims necessity? Well, that's just ridiculous."

Brunelle shook his head, almost impatiently.

"A jury isn't required to believe a defendant, Your Honor. They're not even required to believe either all or none of a defendant's statement. They could believe the part where she admits to killing the victim, but choose not to believe her claim as to why. That's certainly what we're going to ask them to do. But you know what? They don't have to do that either. And you know why? Because they're the jury. They get to decide what the result of this case should be. Not me. Not Ms. Carlisle. Certainly not Ms. Edwards. And not even you, Your Honor. So deny this motion and let the case proceed as it should: to that just result you say I should seek, but which can only truly be secured from a jury. Thank you."

"Wow," Carlisle whispered when he sat down.

"That good?" Brunelle asked.

"That rude," Carlisle replied. "Don't get me wrong. I'm all about being direct, but that's not really your thing. You're more the aw-shucks, simple country lawyer, let's all get along, type. Which is good, because when you try being direct, you just sound like an asshole."

Brunelle frowned, unsure how to reply. But he didn't get a chance anyway, as Judge Gonzalez spoke.

"Thank you, Mr. Brunelle for that... impassioned argument." He turned to the defense table. "Ms. Edwards, I am curious. What was on those CDs that the State provided you at the last hearing? Was there anything that directly supports your client's claim of necessity?"

Edwards stood up. "Well, I don't know, Your Honor. I suppose it depends on whether Mr. Brunelle intends only on introducing clips where the victim seemed relatively lucid while trying to suppress the ones closest in time to the killing, which, I should point out, show him to be far less than completely mentally stable. In my opinion, anyway."

"It's the jury's opinion that matters," Brunelle interjected from his seat. "Which is why it should go to a jury."

Judge Gonzalez's naturally good-natured expression darkened. "Do not interrupt, Mr. Brunelle. And direct your comments to the bench, not opposing counsel. I would expect you to know proper court etiquette after your, lo, so many years as a prosecutor."

Brunelle bit back any defiant reply. He stood up. You always stand up when you address the judge. "Yes, Your Honor.

Sorry, Your Honor."

The judge's expression softened again. "Are you okay, Mr. Brunelle?"

Brunelle sighed again. "I'm fine, Your Honor. Thank you for asking. I just don't have my usual reserves of good will right now. I understand the defense argument. I disagree with it. I expect the Court to deny it, and I guess I just am having trouble slogging through the formalities to get to what seems to me is the only realistic result."

Judge Gonzalez nodded, his frown appearing more one of concern than disapproval. He raised his chin at Brunelle's trial partner. "Is there anything you'd like to add, Ms. Carlisle?"

Carlisle popped to her feet. "Yes, Your Honor. Mr. Brunelle's significant other was hospitalized by a drunk driver last week. I would urge the Court to allow Mr. Brunelle some grace, and look past his demeanor to the merits of his arguments."

"What?" Edwards called out. "Casey? Is she going to be okay?"

"You care about his girlfriend?" Addison blurted. "He's trying to put me in prison."

Edwards looked between her client and her opponent— who was also her friend. "He's just doing his job."

"You should do yours," Addison growled.

"All right, that's enough," Judge Gonzalez interrupted. "You should keep your conversations with your attorney private, Ms. Addison, and privileged." Then he nodded down to Brunelle. "I'm sorry to hear about your significant other, Mr. Brunelle. I hope she's going to be okay."

"She'll live." Brunelle shrugged. "Unlike Mr. Hirsch."

Edwards shook her head. "You're making it easy for me

to agree with my client about you, Dave."

"Enough!" Judge Gonzalez interrupted them. "That's enough. I've heard enough. From both of you."

He took a moment to rub his chin thoughtfully, and to make sure the lawyers were done bickering.

"This is actually a very interesting legal issue," he said. "When can a judge take a case away from a jury? When is it unjust to allow a defendant to face the jeopardy inherent in a verdict on a criminal charge? How much evidence is enough, and which evidence should be considered? All excellent questions... for a law school exam. But as Mr. Brunelle's personal circumstances remind us, we all have a lot of other things on our plate as well. I could spend the morning discussing these lofty legal ideals with some of the most experienced criminal practitioners in the courthouse. Or I could make the obvious ruling and get back to all of the other work already piled up on my desk.

"If it were just me, I might choose the former option," the judge continued. "But it's not just me. Ms. Edwards needs to speak with her client. And Mr. Brunelle needs to attend to his matters as well. So, I will make my ruling: the motion to dismiss is denied. Mr. Brunelle is correct; a jury could choose to believe Ms. Addison's statement that she killed the alleged victim but not believe her explanation as to why. The only way to see if that happens is to allow it to happen. I certainly am not going to stand in the way of that. Motion denied. Court is adjourned."

With that, Judge Gonzalez stood up and his bailiff exhorted everyone else in the courtroom to do the same. Once he was off the bench and safely back in his chambers, Brunelle turned to Carlisle.

"You didn't have to tell the judge about Casey," he complained. "I don't need people to feel bad for me."

Carlisle chuckled and shook her head. "I didn't do it because I wanted the judge to feel bad for you. I did it so we'd win the motion. You were being a jerk and judges like to punish jerks. I gave him the explanation so he couldn't possibly take it out on you. I also saved at least an hour of you and Edwards sniping at each other over the significance of those CDs and the mystery of the missing journal. And I got stuff to do."

Brunelle couldn't help but grin at his partner. "And you feel bad for me."

Carlisle shook her head again, and turned away slightly, avoiding Brunelle's gaze. "I feel bad for Casey," she insisted.

While they were talking, Edwards was having a whispered yet heated discussion with her client, but it was cut short by the guards laying hands on Zoey Addison and escorting her out of the courtroom and back to her cell. Carlisle departed as well, making sure to again comment on how much other work she had to do. The bailiff and the court reporter were also long gone, having followed immediately after Judge Gonzalez. That left Brunelle and Edwards alone in the courtroom.

"Is she going to be okay?" Edwards asked.

Brunelle sighed. "Yeah. Broken femur, some cracked ribs, and a concussion, h   ave. They had to do surgery on the leg, so she's gonʳ

Edwarˑ   ɪn the wall. "Maybe you should take   ɪn her."

Bru   a long drive to Bellevue and back. And sᵖ   ᵉrself okay. She gets tired at night, so I'll be theᵣ

Edwᵃ   ʈhey had known each other for a long time. Long eᵣ   ᵧ honest with each other.

"She's ˑ   ᴀnt, Dave," Edwards insisted. "She really

didn't have any other choice."

Brunelle shook his head. "You keep telling yourself that, Jess," he said, "and you might actually convince yourself."

"I'm going to keep telling *you* that," Edwards replied, "until I actually convince you."

CHAPTER 22

"Did she really say that?" Casey laughed that evening. "Good for her."

"Hm," was all Brunelle managed in response.

"She can be pretty persuasive," Casey continued.

"And I can be pretty stubborn," Brunelle answered. "Irresistible force against immovable object."

"Okay, well, immovable object, would you be willing to move upstairs and grab me an extra blanket?" Casey asked. "I can't seem to get warm."

Casey's house was bigger than Brunelle's condo, but it was also a tri-level, which meant almost everything was not on the same floor as the living room, kitchen, and main bathroom. Casey was camped out on the couch and Brunelle was in charge of fetching and returning anything that was normally kept in the rooms upstairs or downstairs. He had moved a lot of his stuff to the house as well, although there wasn't necessarily space for any of it. Casey's side of the bed had become a makeshift closet for the suits Brunelle pulled off at the end of the workday.

He agreed to fetch the blanket, of course, and spread it

over his girlfriend before slipping into the kitchen to prepare a simple dinner and a couple of homemade cocktails. Dinner had become a lap affair. Casey's leg wasn't ready to make even the small trip to the dining room table. Trips to the bathroom were a struggle enough. It had been a long week.

"Do you think she'll convince the jury?" Casey picked up their conversation after he handed her a plate of chicken and broccoli stir fry. "That's the real question."

Brunelle shrugged. "That's always the question. I can probably block most of her necessity claim from coming out through Chen. Gonzalez wasn't so sure, but I've been doing this a while. That'll force her to put her client on the stand, and then I can cross her."

"She's gonna cry," Casey predicted. "You can't be mean to a woman who's crying on the stand, Dave. The jury will hate you."

"I said I was going to cross-examine her," Brunelle defended. "I didn't say anything about being mean. I can pick apart her defense with a smile on my face."

"What if she stands up to it, though?" Casey continued to play devil's advocate. Or murderer's advocate.

"What if the sun explodes tomorrow?" Brunelle returned with another shrug. "I can't worry about every possibility. I just have to be prepared and deal with stuff as it comes up."

Casey just nodded and took another bite of her dinner. They both chewed in silence for a few moments. Then Casey brought it up finally.

"So, how about that whole pregnancy thing, huh?" she chuckled. "That was weird."

Brunelle felt his heart jump a bit. "Uh, yeah. Totally weird."

Another few moments of quiet.

"I mean, I'm not even sure how I felt about it, you know?" Casey said. "I wasn't really ever planning on being a mom."

"Me either," Brunelle said. "I mean, a dad, but yeah, same."

"Although..." Casey smiled slightly, "I'm kind of surprised that I wasn't scared about it. Like, if we'd gotten that test and it had been positive, that would have been okay, I think, maybe. Right?"

Brunelle had, of course, also thought about all of that. He just hadn't talked about it. Or fully processed it, if he were honest. There had been that whole 'almost killed by a drunk driver' thing in the meantime. But after a moment's thought, he nodded. "Right."

"Really?" Casey leaned forward quickly, then grabbed at her leg. "Ouch. Shit, I gotta move slower. But really? You weren't hoping it was negative?"

Brunelle's mouth knotted. "I'm not sure what I was hoping. Like you said, we weren't planning on kids, and we're both getting kinda old for that shit now."

"Speak for yourself, old man," Casey laughed.

"Ok, I'm getting too old for that," Brunelle amended. "Kids are a lot of work. They change everything."

"Are you afraid of change?" Casey asked.

"It literally took a near death experience to get me to actually move in with you," Brunelle pointed out, "so yeah, maybe."

"Do you like kids?" Casey asked. "We've never really talked about it."

Brunelle wasn't sure. He said as much. "My job doesn't really deal with kids a lot."

"That's a good thing," Casey said. "You don't want to see kids in your line of work."

Then after a moment, she added. "Although you almost did."

Brunelle cocked his head at her. "What do you mean?"

"The Addison case," Casey explained. "If what she said was true, and if she hadn't stopped him, you would have been called out to a playground full of dead kids."

Brunelle set his plate down on his lap. "That's dark."

"It is."

"You should go visit that school," Casey suggested. "See what could have been. If you're going to argue it wasn't true, you should probably know what you're arguing against."

Brunelle knew it was a ploy. Maybe two ploys. The first one was her stated reason. The second one was to get him used to maybe being a dad after all. He was too stubborn to do it for the first reason. But he was willing to do it for the second reason.

"Okay."

CHAPTER 23

It was a sunny day. Still cool in the morning, especially in the shade, before the sun had had the chance to warm the world fully. It reminded Brunelle of the morning of the killing.

Murder, he reminded himself. *Murder is an unlawful killing. It was unlawful because it wasn't necessary.*

He didn't like that he had to remind himself.

He parked his car in front of the rental house where Caleb Hirsch's dead body had blocked the entrance weeks earlier. It didn't look like there were any new renters, probably because of the crime scene tape still posted across the front door. He wondered when Chen might fully release the premises back to the owner. He supposed Chen might be wondering when Brunelle was going to give him the green light for that.

Not yet, he thought.

He stepped out of his car and made his way up the front walk and onto the porch. The cement was still stained from Caleb's blood. That wasn't coming out. They were going to have to paint over it.

He wanted to start where Caleb would have started, if

what Zoey said was true. Brunelle still didn't believe it, but it was undeniably the proper starting point for his excursion.

The school was just up the street. You couldn't quite see it from the porch, but you could hear it, and it came into view as soon as Brunelle reached the sidewalk again. He pushed his hands into his pockets and began a slow walk toward the large, fenced fields of Longfellow Elementary School.

He supposed Caleb, had he actually gone to the school, mass murder on his mind, would have walked faster. But Brunelle wanted to take in the scene. A bright, still cool sun in the sky. Few if any cars driving by. The sounds of children's laughter and screams carried over the crisp breeze. It would have been idyllic for anyone but a murderer. Or a homicide prosecutor.

The school was only three blocks from the house, and they were short blocks. There was a large circular driveway for the school busses and the morning and afternoon drop-off/pick-up lines of parents' cars. The main entrance was just past that, off to one side, marked by the large 'Welcome Leopards!' sign and the flagpole with Old Glory fluttering in the breeze. Brunelle started to cut across the driveway, toward the playground equipment just visible on the other side of the building. It occurred to him that part of Edwards's defense—that is, of Addison's claim—was how feasible the alleged plan of Caleb Hirsch even was. No need to kill him if he wasn't going to succeed anyway.

So far, Caleb would have had to walk past the entire length of the school before he would have gotten to any school kids. Surely someone would have tried to stop him and ask him what he was doing. Then again, no one had tried to stop Brunelle and ask what he was doing.

"Excuse me, sir!" A man's voice rang out behind him. "Can I help you with something?"

Brunelle turned to see the source of the voice. It was a large man in a tightly fitting polo shirt and a pair of pants that probably last fit several years earlier. He was hurrying toward Brunelle from the direction of that main entrance, one thick arm raised in Brunelle's direction. He looked like the vice principal at Brunelle's middle school. He looked like everyone's vice principal at every school.

"No, thanks," Brunelle replied. "I'm just looking around."

The man laughed slightly at that. "This isn't a store, sir. We don't allow unauthorized guests on school property during school hours."

Brunelle was glad to hear that. He might want the jury to hear it too.

"What did you say your name was?" Brunelle asked.

"Well, I didn't," the man replied, "but my name is Andrew Huckleby. I'm the Vice Principal here at Longfellow Elementary."

Of course you are, Brunelle thought.

"Who are you?" Huckleby asked.

"My name is Dave Brunelle. I'm a prosecutor with the King County Prosecutor's Office, and I'm investigating a murder that happened just up the street several weeks ago."

Huckleby's expression changed. He went from potentially menacing to definitely concerned.

"A murder?" he repeated. "I didn't hear anything about that." Then he wondered, "What does that have to do with our school? Was one of our students' families involved? I feel like I would know if one of our students' families was involved."

Brunelle shook his head. "None of your students or their families were involved. At least, we don't believe so."

Huckleby cocked his head. "What does that mean? And

why are you here then?"

"The victim was killed by his girlfriend," Brunelle explained. "She called 911 and waited for the cops to arrive. When they did, she told them she shot him because he was planning on coming here and shooting up the school."

Huckleby's eyes widened. Every Vice Principal's worst fear. Every teacher's worst fear. Every parent's worst fear.

"Did she get arrested?" he asked.

"Yes," Brunelle confirmed.

"Is she in jail right now?"

"Yes."

"Can you do me a favor?" Huckleby asked.

"What?"

"Go into that jail," Huckleby said, "and thank her for me."

Or maybe Brunelle wouldn't be calling him as a witness after all.

"Well, we don't know that any of that is true," Brunelle responded. "It may just have been an excuse to cover up the real reason she killed him."

Huckleby frowned slightly. "Oh. Well, I guess that makes sense."

"And anyway," Brunelle gestured around at the school grounds, "I'm not sure he would have been able to do it anyway. You stopped me as soon as I set foot on school grounds."

Huckleby frowned at him. "You don't have a gun."

That was true, Brunelle supposed. "Do you?" he asked.

"Am I armed with a firearm as I walk around an elementary school?" Huckleby expanded the question with a laugh. "No, I am not. If a gunman came to school, I wouldn't be able to stop him anymore than the kids would."

"Do you have a school safety officer?" Brunelle hoped.

"A uniformed police officer?" Huckleby translated. "Like they have at the high schools? No. Those officers are there primarily to deal with problems caused by the students themselves. We don't need a cop to deal with a seven-year-old stealing tape."

Brunelle definitely didn't want the jury to hear from Vice Principal Huckleby.

"But I'll tell you what," Huckleby continued, "if some bastard did come on to school grounds with the intent to hurt any of my kids, he'd have to use up those bullets on me first. Those are my kids. I would do whatever necessary to protect them."

Necessary. There was that word again.

Huckleby pointed to some kids running around the playground. "You don't seem as concerned about these kids as I think maybe you should be."

"I'm just not sure the killer was as concerned about those kids as she claims she was."

Huckleby crossed his arms and stared down at him. "Do you have kids, Mr. Brunelle?"

Brunelle decided not to recount the whole pregnancy test, drunk driver story. "No, I don't."

Huckleby nodded at him. "That's why you don't believe her."

CHAPTER 24

"Addison didn't have kids either," Carlisle replied when Brunelle told her the story the next day in his office. "We need to keep that vice principal a thousand miles away from the jury."

Brunelle agreed wholeheartedly with that.

"Why did you even go there?" Carlisle asked.

Brunelle hadn't told her yet about the pregnancy scare. Although was it really a 'scare'? he wondered. It was more like a shock. He didn't have enough time to know whether he was scared.

"A trial attorney should always go to the scene of the crime," Brunelle offered his advice.

"The scene of the crime was the house," Carlisle reminded him. "Calling the school 'the scene of the crime' is something Edwards would say."

It was, Brunelle realized. He was going to have to watch that at trial.

"Fine," he said. "The scene of the defendant's bullshit claim of where a crime might have occurred."

Carlisle frowned slightly. "Needs work."

"Yeah," Brunelle had to agree. "Anyway, I wanted to see how feasible it would have been to do what Addison claimed Hirsch was going to do."

"Oh," Carlisle said. "I figured it was so you could decide whether you and Casey wanted to have kids after all. I mean, what with you two thinking she might be pregnant at our dinner and all."

Brunelle's jaw dropped. "How...?"

"You aren't that good at hiding your thoughts, Dave," Carlisle laughed. "And Casey wasn't even trying. You two were dropping little coded references to each other all night, but it was a code like 'one equals A', 'two equals B'. It was pretty obvious."

Brunelle was a bit embarrassed, but there wasn't much to be done about it. "We'll work on a better code next time we talk about it," he offered.

"Next time?" Carlisle cocked her head at him. "So, she is pregnant?"

But Brunelle shook his head. "No. They did a pregnancy screen at the hospital and it came back negative."

"She came in for getting hit by a car, and they gave her a pregnancy test?" Carlisle was incredulous.

"I'm guessing they need to know what kind of medications they shouldn't give or something," Brunelle answered. "That's what they told me. Anyway, she's not pregnant, so we won't even need a code, I guess."

"Unless you two decide to have kids after all," Carlisle pointed out.

Brunelle didn't really want to talk about it anymore right then, so he just replied, "Right."

"So anyway," Carlisle asked, "how feasible was it?"

Brunelle's eyes flew wide. "Getting Casey pregnant?" he

gasped.

"Oh my God, no!" Carlisle recoiled at the suggestion, and the probable image in her mind. "No, the school attack. You said you went there to see how feasible it would have even been to try to kill a bunch of school kids there. How feasible was it?"

Brunelle frowned. "Pretty damn feasible."

Carlisle shrugged. "Well, it doesn't matter. She didn't shoot him at the school. She shot him in the house. He wasn't about to kill anyone there."

"That will need to be our argument," Brunelle remarked, "but it does kind of open a slippery slope. Do we give the jury a map and draw a bunch of lines between the house and the school? She can't shoot him here, but she can here. Here she can stab him. Here she can kneecap him."

"Kneecap?" Carlisle laughed. "What are you, a 1920s gangster?"

"Is it that old of a reference?" Brunelle wondered. "Sounded like 1950s to me."

"Either way, no, no map," Carlisle said. "This isn't about what might have happened. It's about what did happen. She shot and killed him and the only evidence that she had any reason to suspect he was about to commit a greater harm is her own self-serving claims."

Brunelle nodded. "I wish we had that journal."

"You're not the only one." It was Nicole, his paralegal. She was holding a motion in her hand. Again. "I took the liberty of reading it on my way from the front desk where the courier just delivered it."

Brunelle took it, glanced at it, then handed it to Carlisle. "Other shoe."

"Motion to dismiss for failure to preserve exculpatory

evidence," she read aloud. "It should say 'potentially exculpatory'. No one knows if that journal even exists, let alone what's written in it. The legal standard is totally different if the lost evidence is demonstrably exculpatory. This is rank speculation."

Brunelle took it back and looked more closely at it. "It's rank expert opinion. She says she's going to call Young as a witness to testify about what was likely in the journal."

"Shit," Carlisle hissed. "When did she schedule the hearing?"

"One week from today," Brunelle answered. "The minimum time allowed under the court rules."

"You want me to clear your schedule?" Nicole asked.

Brunelle shook his head. "I already did. I was expecting this motion. And I have another thing I need to do too."

CHAPTER 25

Casey wasn't the only one who went to Harborview Hospital that night. And his case hadn't been filed yet, which meant he was still there. Brunelle took some solace in the fact that the drunk driver's injuries were worse than Casey's as he walked into Harborview's main lobby. But not much solace.

The vehicular assault case hadn't been filed yet because the filing of charges started a series of time limits and deadlines. Seventy-two hours from arrest to filing. Fourteen days from filing to arraignment. Sixty days from arraignment to trial. Those were mandatory, established by court rules, statutes, and constitutions, both State and Federal. A defendant could always ask for more time, but not if he was in a coma. The felony traffic prosecutors were right to wait until the driver was well enough to leave the hospital, then arrest and book him into the jail instead. But they had the police reports already. Which meant Brunelle could access them too. And he didn't have any reason to wait.

Patient confidentiality was going to make any inquiries to the hospital reception desk fruitless. But there were other ways to find the driver. Until he was medically approved for discharge, they couldn't risk him slipping out undetected. The cops would be 'sitting on him', the phrase for when a patrol officer was assigned to sit outside the suspect's room, bored out of their mind but pulling their full wages for a day of playing games on their phone, flirting with the nurses, and trying not to fall asleep.

And that cop would be sitting in the hallway where Brunelle could see him. HIPAA didn't prevent him from methodically walking every hallway in the hospital until he saw a Seattle PD officer perched outside of Room W-402.

As Brunelle approached the officer, he checked the white board on the wall next to the door. Written large in the center of the board, its letters scarred with days of sleeves brushing against them as the names of the doctors and nurses at the bottom were updated each day, was the name of the patient: 'DUVALL, G'. That matched the police reports. Gary R. Duvall. Twenty-four years old. No criminal history. Three speeding tickets and one expired tabs violation. Address on file with the Department of Licensing was in Tacoma. He came a long way just to cripple a prosecutor's girlfriend.

"Morning, Officer..." Brunelle squinted at the name patch stitched to the front of the cop's uniform, "...Mendez. How's our patient?"

Brunelle wasn't wearing a police uniform, of course, but he hoped his suit and tie communicated he was a lawyer—no one else in Seattle still wore suits—and his ease with the police that he was a prosecutor. They were on the same team. No secrets among teammates.

"Are you Mr. Brunelle?" Officer Mendez asked.

Brunelle was a bit surprised. He didn't have a name tag on his suit, and he didn't recall encountering Mendez before. Then again, he met a lot of people in his line of work, and one beat cop could look a lot like another.

"Uh, yeah," he answered. "Did we work on a case together?"

Mendez shook his head. "Oh, no. I'm pretty new with the department. Lateral transfer from Renton. But they told me you might try to see the patient. I'm supposed to call Detective Chen if you show up."

Brunelle frowned. *Fucking Larry.*

"That's not really necessary," Brunelle assured. "I just wanted to take a look at him. See how he's doing, you know?"

Mendez shook his head and stood up. He wasn't as tall as Brunelle, but he was thicker. And it wasn't like Brunelle was going to try to force his way past him. Mendez reached for his radio.

"This is Unit 917. Please ask Detective Chen to dispatch to Harborview on the Duvall case. Per previous directive. Over."

"Roger that, 917," came the dispatcher's voice in reply. "Dispatching Chen to Harborview. Over."

Brunelle dropped his head to one side. "Really? So, I can't go in?"

Mendez shrugged. "I'm not sure if you can never go in." He took a step to one side to position himself in front of the door. "But you're not going in until Detective Chen gets here."

Brunelle sighed, but he knew he'd have to wait. And there wasn't even a second chair for him to sit in.

* * *

"Really?" Brunelle threw his hands wide as Chen walked up the hallway some forty minutes later. "I can't take a look at the guy who almost killed my girlfriend?"

"Really," Chen answered. "You're a witness on this one, Dave, not the prosecutor."

"Well, you're not the detective either," Brunelle was certain. "This is the traffic guys, not homicide. No one died, no thanks to that asshole." He pointed at the door Mendez was still standing in front of.

"They knew I was the only one who could say no to you," Chen explained. "The only one you'd listen to anyway."

"What makes you think I'm going to listen to you?" Brunelle challenged.

"Besides getting arrested for obstructing a law enforcement officer if you try anything?"

Brunelle took a moment. "Well, yeah. Besides that."

"Because I am going to let you see him," Chen answered. "With me. You're going to get thirty seconds to look at the bastard, and you're not going to go more than two feet inside the door."

Brunelle crossed his arms. "Afraid I'll try to unplug him?"

Chen just stared at Brunelle.

He dropped his arms again. "Yeah, I might try that. Fuck, Larry. Why are you protecting this guy?"

"I'm protecting the case," Chen answered. "And I'm protecting you."

Chen nodded to Mendez and the officer stepped aside.

"Come on, boyfriend," Chen said to Brunelle, "let's take a look at the guy you want to kill."

Brunelle wished that weren't true. He wished he didn't want Gary Duvall dead for what he did. But he did. He was human, for all the good and bad that meant. Someone hurt someone he cared about. He wanted that person punished.

It was quiet in the room. The monitors hooked up to the bastard were lit up, but not beeping. The sound of the air conditioning filled the space. Brunelle took another step toward the bed, but Chen put an arm out and shook his head. Brunelle had no doubt his friend would arrest him if necessary to protect the integrity of the case.

Duvall's body was limp and amorphous under a stack of thin hospital blankets. His face was bruised and swollen. *Good,* Brunelle couldn't help but think. Other than that, he was just another twenty-something white male, stubble grown out and dirty brown hair pushed back by the nurses. By the time he went on trial, he'd be healed up, clean shaven, with a fresh haircut. His lawyer would probably put him in an argyle sweater too. Anything to make him look young and innocent. It enraged Brunelle.

"Fuck this," Brunelle felt compelled to whisper in the quiet of the room. "Fuck him. And fuck you for getting in the way."

He turned and stormed out of the room, stopping short in the hallway. He wasn't sure anymore why he wanted to see Casey's assailant. He just knew he had to. And he knew he wished he hadn't bothered.

Chen came up behind him and rested a hand on his shoulder. "You're welcome, Dave."

"It wouldn't do any good to kill him now anyway, I suppose," Brunelle mused. "It needed to be before he crested that hill."

"Would you have done it even then?" Chen asked. "Kill a man?"

Brunelle took a moment to really consider the question, and his answer. "Absolutely."

CHAPTER 26

A few days later, Brunelle was in his office just before quitting time. He wasn't working late anymore. Not for a while anyway. Not until Casey could get around a little better. They'd had takeout too many nights in a row, so he was going to hit the grocery store on the way home to pick up a couple of steaks and a fresh bottle of bourbon. Dinner of champions.

But before five o'clock could strike, his boss appeared in his office doorway. Matt Duncan, Elected Prosecutor for King County. Brunelle's boss. The Boss.

"Hey, Dave," Duncan said collegially. He always made sure to talk to his prosecutors collegially. "You got a minute before you head out?"

"Sure," Brunelle answered. Of course. The steaks could wait. "What's up?"

Duncan stepped into the office and sat down in a guest chair across the desk from Brunelle. "I heard you paid a little visit to one of our vehicular assault suspects."

Brunelle frowned. "I didn't take Chen for a snitch," he joked.

"Oh, he's not," Duncan assured. "But he's a cop. A good one. And good cops document everything. Your little visit ended up in a supplemental report that got forwarded to our felony traffic team. They thought I should know."

Brunelle supposed he probably should. "I guess that makes sense. I don't want to risk the prosecution."

"Well, you already tried to do that, Dave," Duncan answered, "but Chen stopped you. If it comes up, the jury will understand. It's only natural to want revenge."

"I just wanted to see him, Matt," Brunelle defended. "I wasn't really going to hurt the guy. I was just hoping he'd hurt himself worse than he hurt Casey."

"Did he?"

"He's still in the hospital and Casey is at home waiting on me to cook her a steak dinner," Brunelle answered, "so I guess so."

"Well, that's something then," Duncan said. "So, I don't have to worry about you involving yourself in the case anymore?"

Brunelle raised his right hand. "Not until I testify at the trial."

"Good." Duncan smiled. Then he nodded at the file open on Brunelle's desk. "Which case are you working on?"

"Woman shoots and kills her boyfriend as he's walking out of the house," Brunelle answered, "then claims she had to because he was going to shoot up a school."

"Oh wow." Duncan nodded thoughtfully. "Was he?"

Brunelle had to shrug. "I don't know. She's the only one who says so, but I don't usually put a lot of stock in what murderers say."

"Of course, if what she says is true..." Duncan started to

point out.

"She's not a murderer," Brunelle finished. "Yeah, I understand that."

"Did you visit the scene?" Duncan asked.

"Yeah. I got there before the victim or the defendant were taken away."

"Did you visit the school?"

"The vice principal wants to give our shooter a medal."

"Did you talk with the victim's psychologist?" Duncan asked. "I assume if there's any truth to what the defendant is claiming, then your victim was seeing a psychologist."

"We spoke with two of them," Brunelle answered. "The one he went to when he was a kid and the one he was seeing up until he was murdered. We also talked with the victim's dad and watched all of his social media clips where he talks about boogie men and secret societies."

"So, there's something to it," Duncan remarked. "Her claim of necessity, I mean."

Brunelle scowled slightly. "Remind me not to let you on the jury."

Duncan laughed. "I wouldn't want to be on that jury. That's going to be a hard decision. What do you think?"

"I'm still prosecuting it," Brunelle answered, "so I guess I think she's lying. Or at least, it wasn't necessity. Either it wasn't as bad as she says, or she should have done something else. You can't just shoot someone in the back six times."

"What would you do if you thought it was justified?" Duncan asked. They both knew the answer.

"I'd dismiss it," Brunelle said. "I'd have to. I can't prosecute someone I think is innocent."

"And what would you need to hear to make you do that?"

Brunelle thought for a moment. "I'm not sure."

Duncan pointed a gentle finger at him. "You should figure that out before the trial starts."

"Why?"

"Because," Duncan answered as he stood to take his leave, "you might just hear it."

CHAPTER 27

Brunelle thought about Duncan's parting words for some time. Duncan was a good boss, a good lawyer, and a good man. But he missed the mark on that one, in Brunelle's opinion. It wasn't just what Brunelle might hear. It was who he heard it from. He'd already heard it from Zoey Addison, but he didn't believe her. He couldn't hear it from Caleb Hirsch because Caleb was dead. That left Dr. John Young. Edwards was going to use the next hearing to try to get the case dismissed. Brunelle was going to use it to see if maybe it should be.

This hearing was scheduled in front of a different judge. Brunelle was glad for that. Judge Gonzalez was pleasant and professional, but Brunelle didn't think it helped his odds to go in front of the same judge three times in a row on motions to dismiss. At some point, smoke added up to fire.

Their new judge was actually one of the oldest judges in the county. Brunelle remembered her when he first started. He was a baby prosecutor handling shoplifts and trespasses, and she was already an experienced judge handling robberies and burglaries. She'd seen it all, including undoubtedly countless variations on the 'I had to do it' defense. Still, this one sat different. Probably because of the children.

"All rise!" the bailiff called out once everyone was assembled in her courtroom. "The King County Superior Court is now in session, The Honorable Susan Jiang presiding."

"Please be seated," Judge Jiang instructed as she did the same herself. "Are the parties ready in the matter of *The State of Washington versus Zoey Addison?*"

They were. Brunelle had coordinated with Carlisle for them to break the plane of the courtroom at 8:59. He didn't want to have to make small talk with Edwards. Not with how he had been in court the last time. And not when she would undoubtedly try to convince him again of her client's innocence. She promised as much the last time they spoke. He didn't want to hear it, in case he heard that thing Duncan was talking about. Although if he was unswayed by what the defendant herself had said, he was unlikely to be persuaded by her paid advocate. There was a reason lawyers were called 'mouthpieces'.

"The State is ready, Your Honor," Carlisle rose to announce. They had decided she would handle the argument. In part, because Brunelle's mood hadn't lifted much since his last caustic remarks to the Court. In part, because Carlisle was his partner on the case and she wanted to do more than just carry his briefcase, as the saying went.

Edwards stood next. "The defense is ready as well, Your Honor."

"Very well," Judge Jiang replied. "I have read the briefing, so unless there are preliminary housekeeping matters, I am ready to hear argument."

"No preliminary matters from the State," Carlisle confirmed.

"Defense?" Judge Jiang raised an expectant eyebrow at Edwards.

"Actually, Your Honor," Edwards raised a finger, "the defense would like to call a witness before arguments."

One of Judge Jiang's eyebrows raised. "A witness? On a purely legal motion? For what purpose? Is there a dispute as to whether the evidence in question was actually preserved?"

"There's no dispute about that," Edwards answered, "but the defense believes the Court would benefit from hearing from the witness because he will be able to explain what information was contained in the missing evidence. That, in turn, goes to the remedy for failing to preserve it, namely dismissal."

Jiang frowned, judicial gears turning behind her eyes. She nodded down to the prosecution table. "Does the State agree, Ms. Carlisle?"

"No, Your Honor, the State does not agree," Carlisle answered. "We think there is a dispute as to whether the evidence in question was not properly preserved because we think there is a dispute as to whether it ever actually existed. However, we have no objection to hearing from the witness we believe Ms. Edwards intends to call. It would be useful to both sides to explore the extent of his knowledge on this subject prior to him testifying at the trial."

"At the trial? You presume you will prevail today, Ms. Carlisle," the judge pointed out.

"I always do, Your Honor," Carlisle replied with a confident nod.

Jiang surrendered the slightest smile at that. "All right then, if there is no objection, I will hear first from the defense's witness. Who is it?"

Edwards straightened up a bit, even as Carlisle sat down

again, and announced formally, "The defense calls Dr. John Young to the stand."

The pomp of the formal announcement was diminished a bit by Edwards then having to leave her client at the defense table, walk to the back of the courtroom, and fetch Dr. Young from where he'd been waiting in the hallway. But after a minute or so, Young entered the courtroom and made his way to the front to be sworn in by the judge.

"Do you swear or affirm that you will tell the truth, the whole truth, and nothing but the truth?" Judge Jiang asked, with her right hand raised as she delivered the oath.

"I do," Young confirmed, his own right hand raised.

"You may take the witness stand," the judge instructed him. Then, to Edwards, "Whenever you're ready, counsel."

"Thank you, Your Honor." Edwards stepped out from behind the defense table again and took up a position at the bar beneath the judge to deliver her questions. "Could you please state your full name for the record, sir?"

"John Logan Young," he answered. He had dressed up for court. No comfortable sweater, although not quite a suit either. He wore dark pants, a brown blazer, and a necktie the color and pattern of mustard and ketchup mixed together. It worked for him.

"How are you employed, Mr. Young?" Edwards didn't say 'Doctor' because she hadn't established that. Very clean advocacy. Brunelle could appreciate it, especially in his role as spectator. Carlisle was far more focused on what was coming after the titles were all established.

"I am a clinical psychiatrist," Young answered. "I own my own practice."

"Do you have any special degrees or training required to

be a clinical psychiatrist?" Edwards continued.

"I do," Young confirmed. "I have a Bachelor of Science Degree in biology and organic chemistry from the University of California at Irvine and a Medical Doctorate degree from the University of Washington. I completed a four-year residency at Benedictine Hospital in Portland, Oregon. Three of those years were in psychiatry."

"How long have you been practicing as a clinical psychiatrist?" Edwards asked next.

Young took a moment to do the math. "Twenty-one years now. Wow. I didn't realize it had been quite so long."

"Almost ready to retire, huh?" Edwards joked. Nothing wrong with taking a moment to build rapport with your witness.

"No, not quite yet," Young answered. "I'm fortunate to love what I do. I can't imagine retiring. Ask me again in ten years."

"Well, hopefully, I won't be seeing you again in ten years," Edwards replied. "At least not in this type of setting. But speaking of that, let's get to the reason you're here today, shall we? Did you have a patient by the name of Caleb Hirsch?"

Young nodded solemnly. "I did."

"Is this the same Caleb Hirsch," Edwards needed to make the record clear, "who died as a result of the circumstances in this criminal case?"

Is this the same Calen Hirsch my client murdered? Brunelle translated in his head.

"Yes," Young confirmed.

"How long was Caleb a patient of yours?" Edwards asked.

"Not terribly long, I'm afraid," Young answered. "Less than a year. I wish he'd come to me sooner. I might have been able to prevent all this."

Nice opening for Edwards, Brunelle knew. Edwards knew it too, of course.

"How could treating Caleb," she asked, "have prevented Zoey from shooting him that morning?"

Young frowned and shifted his weight in the chair. "Well, you see, I was treating Caleb for the recent onset of what appeared to be paranoid schizophrenia, along with some attendant personality issues. As I understand it, Ms. Addison told the police that she shot Caleb because he was about to act on a paranoid delusion. Act violently, I mean."

Edwards nodded. "That is what she told police. Does that seem credible to you?"

"Objection!" Carlisle stood up. "I would object to the form of the question. One witness is not permitted to give an opinion as to the truthfulness of another witness."

Judge Jiang nodded reluctantly. No one enjoyed testimony being interrupted, least of all the person who was supposed to make a decision based on it. But Carlisle wasn't wrong. "Can you rephrase, Ms. Edwards?"

"Of course, Your Honor," Edwards replied evenly. Carlisle sat down again.

"Dr. Young," Edwards asked, "Ms. Addison's statement to the police that Caleb told her he was going to murder school children across the street, would that be medically consistent with your clinical impressions of Caleb Hirsch?"

Young nodded. "It would."

"Please explain why you think that," Edwards instructed.

Young took a moment to gather his thoughts, then launched into the explanation. "As I mentioned, I was treating Caleb for paranoid schizophrenia. Prior to coming to see me,

Caleb's condition had been limited to potential personality disorders during his teenage years. However, schizophrenia commonly manifests in early adulthood. He began to have invasive thoughts and even delusions. He delayed seeking help, but eventually contacted his old therapist who sent him to me. Once I realized what we were probably dealing with, I prescribed antipsychotics, but it can take a while to find the right balance of medication. There's a lot of trial and error to see what works, and what side effects are tolerable. There are always side effects. In the meantime, as we worked on getting the medications right, we also participated in traditional psychotherapy sessions. Talk therapy, people sometimes call it. And it was in those sessions that I learned some of the delusions he was suffering from."

"What delusions was he suffering from, Doctor?" Edwards prompted.

"Generally, he had a feeling that he was being monitored," Young answered. "That's a fairly common delusion among cases of paranoid schizophrenia. Indeed, that's the main symptom that differentiates it from other forms of schizophrenia. More specifically, he was starting to suspect that the people nearest to him were agents of some ill-defined organization that was keeping him under observation, for some, as yet undetermined purpose."

"People like Zoey?" Edwards asked.

"Interestingly, no," Young answered. "He trusted Zoey very deeply. He saw her as an ally in the battle to come. No, when I said 'nearest', I meant geographically near. He thought the people who were observing him were taking up positions near his home in order to keep him under constant observation. Unfortunately, he started to believe that included the children at the school up the street."

"Your Honor, I'm going to have to object again," Carlisle interjected. "All of this will be of great interest to the jury at trial, I'm sure, but none of it goes to the defense claim that the State failed to preserve exculpatory evidence, unless Ms. Edwards expects to have this witness testify that the police destroyed his records regarding Mr. Hirsch or some similarly outlandish claim."

Judge Jiang frowned again. Judges frowned a lot. She looked down to Edwards. "Is this going somewhere relevant to today's motion, Ms. Edward?"

"Yes, Your Honor," Edwards answered, "but I can move along a bit." She turned back to the witness. "Doctor, as part of your therapy with Caleb, did you ask him to keep a journal?"

Young nodded. "I did."

"What sorts of things did you ask him to record in his journal?"

"Well, he could include anything he felt was important, of course," Young answered, "but what I was primarily interested in was any intrusive or potentially delusional thoughts."

"What would be the purpose of recording those thoughts?" Edwards asked.

"The first purpose would be for me to know them," Young answered. "Patients don't always remember everything that happens between sessions. In fact, there's usually too much to discuss in one session anyway. The journal would serve as a way for me to see what sorts of things he was experiencing away from therapy, as they happened."

"You said that was the first purpose," Edwards said. "What are the other purposes?"

"It would allow me to track changes in thinking," Young explained, "and share those changes with Caleb. Everyone thinks their current thoughts are normal and justified. Not just people with mental illness, all of us. When you're angry or sad or elated, you feel like you have reasons to feel that way, even if those around you wonder why you're so upset about something they think is trivial. Coming back to certain thoughts after they've receded can help the patient see that sometimes those feelings weren't so appropriate after all."

"Anything else?" Edwards asked.

"I think the third important purpose is just record keeping," Young said. "There's no better information than information directly from the patient, and there's no better way to preserve that than to write it down."

Edwards grinned at that answer. "So, it's important to preserve that information?"

"Vitally important, yes," Young agreed.

"So, where is that journal now?"

Young shrugged. "I don't know."

"You don't know?" Edwards feigned surprise.

"No," Young confirmed. "Caleb kept the journal with him. He was supposed to write thoughts down as they happened, so it wouldn't do any good if I kept it at my office. He would bring it with him to session, then take it with him again when he left."

"So, the journal would have been at his residence?" Edwards asked.

"Objection!" Carlisle interrupted again. "Calls for speculation."

Judge Jiang nodded. "Sustained. Ask it a different way, Ms. Edwards."

Edwards thought for a moment. "I don't think I need to, Your Honor. I've made my point. No further questions."

She returned to her seat next to Addison and Carlisle

stood up. Time for cross-examination.

They had decided to have Carlisle handle the witness in part because she hadn't done much in court up to that point. But the other reason was that she was more aggressive than Brunelle, more cutting, and more precise. She was right; Brunelle was 'aw shucks'. Carlisle was 'take that'.

"You don't know where Calen Hirsch kept his journal, do you?"

"No, I don't," Young agreed.

"But every week, as part of your therapy sessions, you read what was in that journal, didn't you?"

"I did," Young agreed again.

Cross-examination was all about forcing the witness to agree with you. *Lead, lead, lead the witness,* was what they taught at trial skills seminars. Tell them the answer and make them agree. Hit hard. Hit fast. Sit down.

"So, while the journal itself may have been lost," Carlisle put to him, "the information in the journal is available through you—your memory and your clinical notes. Isn't that true?"

Young hesitated. "For the most part. I can't guarantee I can remember every single thing in them. But yes, I did review them every time we met."

That was enough, Brunelle felt. Carlisle had established what they needed to survive the motion: (1) there was no evidence the journal was even in the residence the police searched, and (2) any information that might have been in the journal was available through Young and therefore not actually lost. But Carlisle was good enough to know the judge would want one more piece of information.

"And there was nothing in that journal, ever, about killing the school children across the street," she said. "Was there, doctor?"

"No," Young agreed. "There was not. I didn't know."

That last bit was why Carlisle knew Young would agree with her. He didn't know. It wasn't his fault. He didn't want it to be his fault.

"No further questions," Carlisle announced, and returned to the prosecution table.

Brunelle tried to offer a whispered compliment, but she shushed him, her eyes intent on Edwards rising from her seat for redirect-examination.

"How long was it between your last session with Caleb Hirsch," Edwards asked, "and his death, Doctor?"

Young took a moment to think. "Approximately ten days. We were meeting every other week and he had an appointment coming up."

"Approximately ten days," Edwards replied. "And so that's ten days of journal entries you never saw, correct?"

"Correct," Young agreed.

"The ten days immediately preceding the incident on this case," Edwards said.

'Incident'. Brunelle rolled his eyes at the euphemism.

"Probably the ten most important days in this entire case," Edwards asserted, "if we want to understand exactly what Caleb was thinking prior to the morning he told Zoey he was going to murder those school children."

"Objection." Carlisle rose once again. "There's been no testimony at this hearing that Mr. Hirsch ever actually said anything of the sort to the defendant."

Judge Jiang was tiring of the lawyers. Judges did that a lot too. "I'm going to overrule the objection. I understand what is being asked. You may answer the question, Doctor, if you're able."

"I would agree that any journal entries from those days would shed light on Caleb's thinking prior to the day of his death," Young answered. "If he made any entries."

Edwards frowned slightly at the qualification. "Well, he was supposed to record all of his invasive thoughts, wasn't he?"

"He was." Young grinned slightly. "But he didn't always. Do you always do everything you're supposed to do?"

Edwards didn't answer the question. She was supposed to be posing them.

"I knew he didn't always write everything down," Young continued. "Sometimes he wanted to keep things from me. That was part of his condition. That was why we would discuss them, instead of him just handing them in like a homework assignment. If he really did have a sudden decline that led to homicidal ideation, I don't know that he would have put that in writing."

Brunelle grinned to himself at that. Edwards made a mistake they also taught you to avoid at those seminars: asking one question too many.

Flustered, but unsure how to recover, she waved her hand at nothing in particular and conceded, "All right then. No further questions."

Carlisle could have conducted recross-examination, and in front of a jury she might have, just to make sure they understood the import of what Young had just said. But it was a judge who would be making the decision that day, and there was no doubt Judge Jiang had understood it.

"No recross, Your Honor," Carlisle announced.

That ended the good doctor's testimony. The judge excused him and he made his way out of the courtroom, free to go back to work. It wasn't Monday.

"Any further witnesses, Ms. Edwards?" Judge Jiang inquired.

"No, Your Honor," Edwards answered. "The defense rests."

"Any witnesses for the State, Ms. Carlisle?" the judge had to ask.

"No, Your Honor." Carlisle gave the answer everyone knew she would. "We're ready to proceed to argument."

Jiang nodded. She was ready too. "As I said at the beginning of the hearing, this is the defense's motion, so I will hear first from them. Whenever you're ready, Ms. Edwards."

Edwards was whispering with her client following the conclusion of their witness's testimony, but she cut it short and stood to address the Court.

"Thank you, Your Honor. Dr. Young's testimony established two things beyond any doubt. First, the alleged victim in this case suffered from the exact sort of mental illness my client described to the police. And second, that he was recording his impacted thoughts in a written journal. It is also without a doubt that the police never recovered this journal. They failed to preserve vital evidence in this case. Indeed, I would submit that Mr. Hirsch's journal is the single most important piece of evidence in this entire case." She pointed at Brunelle and Carlisle. "And they lost it."

Edwards came out from behind the defense table. It was a normal move in front of a jury. In front of a judge, it was a bit aggressive. Confident, perhaps. Or maybe just desperate.

"This entire case is going to come down to whether the jury believes the defense of necessity has been proven," Edwards continued. "It's important to note that necessity is an affirmative defense. It's not like self-defense, which is an implied element of the offense that the State has to prove the absence of, beyond a reasonable doubt. That might change the analysis. If the State fails to preserve evidence they need to address in order to prove the charge, then they are also victims of that negligence. But with necessity, the State first proves the underlying charge, and then the defense has to put forward evidence to prove the defense. Well, how am I supposed to do that when they didn't collect the one piece of independent evidence that would help establish the defense? Sure, Ms. Addison can take the stand and tell them what happened, what Caleb told her, that she had no choice."

Again a gesture at the prosecution table. "But what are they going to do? They're going to tell the jury not to believe her. That she's making excuses after the fact. That she would say anything to avoid punishment. To get away with murder. And the jury will probably believe that. But the State wouldn't be able to make that argument about the victim's own words, recorded maybe even the night before his girlfriend faced the impossible choice of stopping him or allowing the unthinkable to happen.

"The prosecutors can't tell the jury to ignore the words of their own victim," Edwards argued. "And that's why we don't have the journal. Or at least that's why they seem so unbothered by its absence. They were in no hurry to seek out exculpatory evidence, and by the time Dr. Young told them about the journal, the crime scene had long since been processed and released. But no big deal for them. It only would have helped the defense anyway."

Edwards took a step back and placed a hand on the table behind her. "Now, they may argue that the defense can still produce the information in the journal to the jury via Dr. Young, but he admitted just now that he didn't see the journal entries from the ten days immediately prior to Mr. Hirsch attempting to murder a schoolyard full of children. Those are lost forever, and it's the State's job to find, collect, and preserve such evidence. They have an obligation not to always win the case, Your Honor. They have an obligation to the truth. And the truth is, my client acted in necessity that morning. But my ability to prove that defense at trial has been irreparably damaged by the State's failures. Ms. Addison has no redress to the jury. But she has redress to this Court, Your Honor. She has redress to you. And we implore you to do the right thing. Hold the State to all of their obligations and not just the ones that help their case, and dismiss this case. Thank you."

Edwards came back around the table and sat down next to her client, who seemed appreciative of her efforts, if not perhaps convinced. Brunelle hoped Jiang wasn't convinced either. Carlisle would try to make sure of that.

"Ms. Carlisle?" the judge invited. "Whenever you're ready."

Carlisle stood to address the Court from her spot behind the prosecution table. She wasn't going to make it weird by stepping into the judge's bubble, which at that point in the hearing extended over pretty much the entire courtroom.

"Thank you, Your Honor. I'll be brief." Carlisle began. "The journal in question was never collected by the police. They cannot have failed to preserve something they never possessed. If the facts surrounding this journal were different—if they had collected it at the crime scene but lost it between there and the property room—then the defense motion might have some merit. But here, the police collected all of the evidence they located at the scene and all of that evidence has been properly preserved and is still stored in the Seattle Police Department property room."

It was Carlisle's turn to gesture at her opponent.

"Defense is asking the Court to extend the law regarding losing evidence to the situation when evidence is never located in the first place. That is not the law, and indeed it cannot be. Would the State have preferred it if that journal had been located? Of course. Would we evaluate any evidence in it professionally and fairly, even if it benefitted the defendant? Absolutely. And any suggestion to the contrary is, quite honestly, Your Honor, offensive. We are fully aware of our ethics. We know that we must not prosecute innocent people, and a person who truly acts in accordance with the elements of the necessity defense is not guilty. That is the law and we are devoted to upholding the law.

"But speculation of what might have been in that journal is not evidence. Wishful thinking by the defense attorney is not evidence. What is evidence is that Zoey Addison shot and killed Caleb Hirsch. What is evidence is that there was no one in that house in any immediate danger of anything. Not even the defendant claimed she was acting in self-defense. The police collected all of the available evidence. The State and the defense disagree on the import of that evidence, but we will each argue the evidence to the jury, and the jury will make a decision. That is how the system works. Let the system work. Deny the defense motion to dismiss. Thank you."

Judge Jiang nodded and leaned back in her chair. "First of all, let me say that I appreciate well-reasoned arguments from experienced, articulate counsel. I also appreciate it when the lawyers avoid unnecessary attacks on opposing counsel. The nature of this argument requires, I think, some allegation of wrongdoing by at least one side, but it didn't devolve into name-calling. So, again I appreciate that."

Brunelle wondered why judges always took so long to

make their rulings. Most lawyers, having completed their work, would probably have preferred a simple 'Granted' or 'Denied', maybe with an accompanying thumb pointing up or down, to the rambling of the judge as to how they reached whatever ruling they were going to reach. He suspected it was because most of them weren't one hundred percent certain how they were going to rule until they heard their own reasoning. Everyone assembled was forced to hear the judge's thought process as the decision was arrived at. That was probably half of it, Brunelle figured. The other half was just that judges liked hearing themselves talk.

"I think we are all in agreement," Judge Jiang continued, "that this journal would have been a valuable piece of evidence to collect. It would have provided some definitive evidence regarding the defendant's claim of necessity. I am convinced of that. I believe Ms. Carlisle when she says the State would act appropriately on whatever the contents of the journal might have been. But I'm not sure that I'm convinced the information would necessarily have benefited one party or the other."

Jiang's mouth twisted into a thoughtful knot and she gestured vaguely at the empty witness stand. "Dr. Young indicated that Mr. Hirsch was indeed having the sort of paranoid delusions the defendant claimed he told her of the morning of the killing. But he was unable to confirm anything as specific as what the defendant told the police. More importantly, I think, he indicated that Mr. Hirsch didn't always put everything in the journal that he was supposed to. Had the journal been found, it might not have contained the evidence the defense asserts would have been there. The defense would then have to rely on Dr. Young's opinion that its absence in the journal does not necessarily mean it was absent from the defendant's mind. Both sides would have to argue inferences from the contents of the journal, not different from having to argue inferences from Dr. Young's testimony, the defendant's statement to the police, or the physical evidence at the scene."

The judge gestured at both counsel tables simultaneously. "That's what lawyers do. And I am going to let you do it. The motion to dismiss is denied. The case is confirmed for trial."

Brunelle turned to Carlisle. "Good job."

Carlisle kept her eyes on the judge. "I know."

"Trial is scheduled to begin two weeks from Monday," the judge continued, glancing at the information on the computer screen jammed into the corner of her work area atop the bench. "Will both parties be ready on that date?"

The prosecutor usually answered the judge first, but Edwards broke protocol, probably because she was frustrated with the Court's ruling. "The defense will be ready, Your Honor."

Judge Jiang nodded at Edwards, then looked expectantly to Carlisle. She raised her chin and answered for the State.

"Yes, Your Honor. We're ready."

CHAPTER 28

Brunelle left the office early the following Monday afternoon, after a weekend of obsessing on the case even as he doted on Casey. His early departure wasn't a reward to himself for their victory over Edwards. It was in spite of it. They had won in front of the judge, but Brunelle wasn't convinced they would do so in front of the jury. Edwards raised good points when she said Caleb's journal could have been exculpatory. Judge Jiang raised a better one when she suggested it might not have been.

Brunelle wanted that journal. And even though Caleb and Zoey's house was the opposite direction of his drive 'home' to Casey's place, he couldn't walk into trial without trying himself to find what Edwards rightly called 'the most important piece of evidence in the case'.

The only problem was, he didn't have a key. But Chen did. And he could hardly exclude Carlisle. What kind of partner would that have made him? So, at 4:30, the three of them met at the scene of the crime, Chen with the key, Brunelle with the hope, and Carlisle with the snark.

"You really think you're better at this than the cops?" she

asked Brunelle. "I mean, better than Larry? Sure. But there were lots of cops there that day, right? They couldn't all be as incompetent as you two."

"That's why you're here," Brunelle returned. "Just to prove you're as incompetent as the two of us."

"Wanna bet who grabs the journal first?" Carlisle challenged.

"Neither of you grab anything," Chen instructed. "You don't touch evidence. I do. If you find something, you tell me and I collect it. Is that understood?"

Carlisle frowned. "You're no fun."

"I'm a detective," Chen replied. "And I am delight itself."

That seemed unlikely, especially in that moment, but Brunelle decided not to keep the riff going.

Chen unlocked the door and flipped the light switch on the wall. "Knock yourself out. We searched this place top to bottom, twice. Absent a wardrobe to a perennial winterscape, you're not going to find anything new."

Brunelle took it as a warning, but Carlisle flashed a smile that showed she took it as a challenge.

"Let's meet back here in thirty minutes," Brunelle suggested, "unless someone finds something sooner."

"See you in thirty minutes," Chen replied immediately.

"Party pooper," Carlisle teased him. Then she disappeared into the house.

"Do you really think you're going to find it?" Chen asked Brunelle.

He thought for a moment, then admitted, "No. But I really want to. And I won't be able to focus on the rest of the evidence until I've confirmed for myself that there is no journal."

Chen waved his hand toward the interior of the house.

"Be my guest. I'll wait here. I'm just the guy with the key."

Brunelle could hardly blame Chen for his sour mood. Two lawyers were implicitly telling him they could be better detectives than him. Brunelle justified the excursion on the basis that they had additional information since the morning of the murder and even since Chen went back after they first learned about the journal from Young. Brunelle wasn't entirely sure what that new information was, other than maybe Young testifying that Caleb might not have included anything important anyway. If that was true, there was less need to stash it away. Maybe it was hiding in plain sight.

Despite that logic, Brunelle spent his time in the bedroom, searching for secret hiding places. The truth was, if it had been hiding in plain sight, the cops would have found it. 'Plain sight' was an actual legal doctrine in search warrant law. Things in plain sight were observed, not overlooked. That only left hiding places.

Brunelle checked everywhere he could think of. Behind the headboard. The underside of the bedside tables. He even unscrewed the faceplates covering the outlets, theorizing Caleb could have perhaps transferred the contents of the journal to a thumb drive. But no luck. The thirty minutes was almost up, and he knew Carlisle hadn't found anything either. If she had, they all would have known about it immediately.

For his last desperate attempt, Brunelle laid on his back and scooted as far as he could under the bed. Maybe the journal was tucked between the slats of the bed frame and the mattress. It was not, he confirmed, but he found something that gave him a spark of hope, if only momentarily. On the underside of the bed slats, right next to the headboard, there were a series of brass brackets that could have served as a place to slide something about the size of a typical journal. There was no journal there then, though. Nothing but empty brackets. And time was up.

Brunelle pulled himself out from under the bed. Weeks without inhabitants had allowed the dust to pile up and he found himself brushing off surprisingly sticky grime from his pants as he rejoined Chen and Carlisle in the front entryway.

"Find anything?" he asked Carlisle.

She shook her head with a frown. "Nope. What about you?"

"Nothing," Brunelle replied. "I did find a place it could have been, though."

"Those brackets under the bed frame?" Chen asked. When Brunelle nodded, he added, "Yeah, I saw those too. I looked into it and it's supposed to be where you store the assembly instructions after you put the bed together at home with an Allen wrench and a miniature bottle of wood glue."

"I hate furniture like that," Carlisle grumbled. "I mean, I buy it because its's way cheaper, but I hate it."

Brunelle considered the empty brackets. "The instructions weren't there."

"Do you ever keep the instructions after you assemble the furniture?" Chen asked.

"I don't," Carlisle answered.

Brunelle didn't either. "So, nothing then?" he asked in confirmation.

"Did you find anything, Larry?" Carlisle asked Chen.

"Yeah, I found a couple of hundred things when we were first called out," he answered. "But nothing since, because we found it all the first time."

Brunelle shrugged. "Well, at least I can rest easy that the journal really isn't hiding here somewhere. We can go forward confidently without it."

But a frown crept into the corner of his mouth as they departed and Chen locked the door behind them.

They were going forward to trial. But he didn't feel confident.

CHAPTER 29

There being no new evidence to provide to defense, the final week before trial was consumed with the administrative tasks necessary to be fully prepared once the proceedings began. They needed clean copies of each photograph to mark and admit to the jury. They needed clean copies of each police report for the cops to have in front of them when they testified, in case they needed to refresh their recollection about what exactly they saw and did. They needed to call each witness to confirm availability one last time and talk scheduling. Cops had kids with doctor appointments too.

Brunelle and Carlisle also met several times to go over the evidence again and divide up the portions of the trial each of them would do. Brunelle would do the opening statement. Carlisle would do the closing argument. Those were different in kind and that division worked to their strengths. They also divvyed up the witnesses. Cops and forensics, psychiatrists and medical examiners, family and vice principals. Thanks to Carlisle, they had everything ready two days before the trial started. That allowed them to relax the day before. Or steel themselves anyway.

Every trial attorney had their own routine the night before trial. Brunelle didn't know what Carlisle's was, and he wasn't particularly curious either. He knew it didn't involve him and that was enough. He himself preferred to spend the night before trial alone, just him, his thoughts, the lights from downtown from his balcony, and a single glass of 10-year-old bourbon.

Unfortunately, he was ten miles from downtown Seattle, not alone, his thoughts unavoidably intertwined with Casey and hers. At least he had the bourbon.

"Can you grab me another pillow?" Casey asked, struggling to sit more comfortably. "I am so sick of this couch."

"Of course," Brunelle answered, almost reflexively. He disappeared to the bedroom, then returned with two pillows and a blanket. He didn't want to go back again, if he could avoid it.

"Anticipating my needs," Casey observed. "I approve."

Brunelle just smiled and nodded. He sat down again on the chair next to his bourbon.

"Thinking about the trial?" Casey asked as she jammed a pillow behind her back. "I can't blame you. Are you ready?"

Brunelle nodded, but again, almost reflexively. "Yep."

"Do you have a good response to that necessity defense?" Casey asked.

Brunelle shook his head. "Nope. Just that it's self-serving bullshit and you should never believe a defendant."

Casey took a moment before speaking again. "I'm sorry I told you I believed her when the case started. I know you wouldn't prosecute a case if you didn't think it was the right thing to do."

Another reflexive nod. "Thanks." But his eyes were unfocused and his mind distant.

"You want to watch a movie or something?" Casey suggested. "Take your mind off of it? Unless you want to think about it. Obsess all night, get no rest, and show up for trial exhausted and sluggish."

Brunelle smiled absently. "Sure. A movie sounds good."

Casey grabbed the remote control from the table with a wince. "What do you want to watch?"

"You choose," Brunelle answered. He got up from the chair and transported himself and his bourbon to the floor in front of the couch.

Casey ran fingers through his hair as she navigated the on-screen menu. "Are you sure this is all right? I know it's not what you usually do the night before trial."

"Things change," he replied. "That's how life is, right? You adjust and you adapt and you do what you have to."

"Necessity, huh?" Casey joked.

Brunelle stifled a sigh with a sip of bourbon. "Sure. Something like that."

CHAPTER 30

The first day of trial was always a bit like running in sand. Slower going than you expected, even though you should have expected the going to be exactly that slow. There were all the administrative and housekeeping matters to attend to, the first of which was receiving the assignment of judge. King County Superior Court had 53 different judges, any of whom might be already tied up in a trial or might have become available because a trial just ended, either in normal course or due to some unexpected event, like a mid-trial plea bargain. Brunelle would have been fine with either Judge Gonzalez or Judge Jiang. Instead, they got Judge Doyle.

"Ugh," Carlisle said as they walked to Doyle's courtroom. "I hate Doyle. There's nothing worse than a judge who thinks he's the smartest person in the room."

"Especially when he's actually dead last in that department," Brunelle added knowingly.

Doyle had been appointed into a vacancy created by a retiring judge, and no one had wanted to run against an incumbent in the following election. Doyle had taken it as a validation of his judicial prowess, when really it was the reality of the professional world they inhabited. No lawyer wanted to spend tens of thousands of dollars of their own money to try to take a judge's job away from them, only to lose because of the power of incumbency and then have to appear in front of that judge again as a lawyer. Better to wait for an open seat or seek an appointment at the next vacancy. So, Doyle was an average lawyer at best, but thought of himself as the greatest of judges. It was just one more thing to navigate during a trial filled with unexpected eddies and currents.

"Could have been worse," Carlisle tried.

Then they both said, "Could have been better," at the same time, and laughed. At least they were in sync.

Edwards was already inside the courtroom when they arrived, her client next to her, dressed out in street clothes. No jail scrubs during the trial. The jury wasn't allowed to know a defendant was being held on bail. It put a crimp on that whole 'presumed innocent' thing. But there were two armed corrections officers in the courtroom as well, stationed at the exits, so the sharper jurors could probably figure it out anyway.

Brunelle would have been fine to skip anything more than the barest of greetings with Edwards. He was trying to get into the proper headspace for trial. Spending the night before, and every night coming up, having to talk with someone rather than decompress on his own wasn't helping. Friendly banter with his opponent wasn't going to help either. But Edwards had different ideas.

"Morning, Gwen. Hey, Dave," she said, stepping up to Brunelle as he and Carlisle reached the prosecution table. "How's Casey doing?"

Brunelle sighed. He didn't want to talk, but he wasn't

going to be a jerk about it. "She's healing up. The doctor said it was going to take a few months, and it looks like they were right."

"That sucks," Edwards said. "But I heard they filed vehicular assault charges on the guy who did it. He was finally recovered enough to leave the hospital."

"Huh," Brunelle replied. He wasn't going to tell her about his trip to visit Mr. Duvall. "I've been too focused on this case to worry about that one."

"It's not too late to free yourself up, Dave," Edwards finally got to it. "You know your case is weak and you know why. My client really did have no choice. At least, that's what she thought in the moment. She's not guilty. You can dismiss it right now, and get back to taking care of Casey."

"Casey can take care of herself," Brunelle returned. That was mostly true, although she was still weeks away from being able to walk on her own. "I'm not going to dismiss a murder case—or any case, for that matter—for my own personal convenience. I thought you knew me better than that, Jess."

Jess nodded. "Yeah, you're right. I do," she allowed. "But I also know you well enough that you want to do the right thing. I'll admit most of the time that means a conviction, no matter what I say during the trial. But this case is different. I'm surprised you don't see that."

"You haven't shown me anything to make me see it," Brunelle answered. "Your client shot her boyfriend in the back inside their own home. I just can't buy some story about saving school kids ten blocks away."

"It's three blocks, Dave," Edwards responded. "I'm sure you know that. You probably walked it yourself to be sure."

Brunelle sighed. Again, he didn't want to be a jerk about it, but he needed to focus on the job ahead of him. "Do you have anything else, Jess? Anything new? Because if not, I need to get ready to pick a jury."

"I guess not, Dave," Edwards admitted. "But you know how trials are. Anything can happen. Just promise me you'll keep an open mind and if you finally believe me and my client, you'll do the right thing."

Brunelle stared at his erstwhile opponent for several seconds. "I promise I will do the right thing."

"Me too!" Carlisle piped in, with a wave and a broad grin. "Nice talk, Jess. See you at closing arguments."

Judge Doyle took the bench shortly thereafter. Again, he wasn't unpleasant, just dense. It meant that run in the sand would be even slower.

"Are the parties ready on the matter of *The State of Washington versus Zoey Claire Addison*?" he asked following the bailiff's call to rise upon his entrance. He was on the younger side for a Superior Court judge, still in his forties, with thin black hair in a conservative cut, angular features, and a five o'clock shadow already starting at 9:02 a.m.

"The State is ready, Your Honor," Brunelle confirmed, standing out of due respect for the position at least.

"The defense is ready as well, Your Honor," Edwards answered.

"Excellent." Doyle rubbed his hands together. "Let's get started. I'm excited to preside over a murder trial."

The first item on the pre-flight checklist was scheduling. Comparing any unavoidable conflicts the attorneys might have with any similar conflicts of the Court. Next were any evidence issues that needed to be resolved prior to speaking with potential jurors. Thanks to Edwards's multiple motions to dismiss, most of the evidentiary issues had already been resolved. It wasn't like they had a journal to redact anyway. Then came the parameters for picking the jury. They needed twelve to render a verdict, but they would need to seat alternate jurors as well, in case any of the main twelve became unable to serve over the several weeks the trial was certain to last. Brunelle suggested four alternates; Edwards suggested one. They did so for the same reason: if they dropped below twelve jurors, it would be a mistrial and they'd have to start all over again. Defense attorneys called mistrials 'temporary dismissals'. Judge Doyle split the difference at three alternates, which was what Brunelle expected and why he proposed four.

The jury panel—'venire' for the lawyers who still preferred to use inaccessible legal jargon—was one hundred potential jurors. One hundred, because many of them would have personal or professional conflicts that would prevent them from sitting on such a long trial. Several more of them would have personal connections or experiences that made it inappropriate for them to sit in that particular trial. Maybe they knew one of the witnesses. Maybe someone in their family had been the victim of the same or similar crime, or even had committed it. Once all of those jurors were identified and examined and excused, then the remainder of the panel would be considered for the actual jury. They were numbered from 1-100, and the first twelve were the presumptive jury, with the next three being the alternates. But after the attorneys took turns questioning them as a group, thirty minutes per side, as many rounds as they needed, some of those first fifteen would be stricken, by one side or the other or even the judge, for any number of reasons that were impossible to predict.

The entire process of selecting, empaneling, and swearing in the final jury took over a week itself. But eventually the time came when those fifteen upstanding citizens took their seats in the jury box and Judge Doyle announced the start of the actual trial.

"Ladies and gentlemen of the jury," he instructed, "please give your attention to Mr. Brunelle, who will deliver the opening statement on behalf of The State of Washington."

CHAPTER 31

Brunelle stood up, buttoned his suit coat, and stepped out from behind the prosecution table. He took up his usual spot directly in front of the center of the jury box, close enough to communicate confidence but not so close as to make the jurors uncomfortable. The courtroom was silent. Everyone was waiting on the first official words of the trial. The words of the prosecutor. His words.

He had spent a lot of time thinking about this exact moment. He knew he would never have the jury's attention more than he had it at that exact moment. He couldn't squander it. But every case was different and this one was particularly troublesome. He didn't have to prove Zoey Addison didn't act in necessity. Edwards had to prove that she did. So it wasn't his burden and technically he didn't even have to mention it. But Edwards would, which meant he had to do it first. The lawyers called it 'drawing the sting'. Because as bad as something might seem for your case, it seemed doubly so if you looked like you were trying to hide it.

So Brunelle had to draw the sting. But he had to do more.

He had to define that sting before Edwards got the chance to say even one word to the jurors.

"Victim blaming," Brunelle began. "That's what it's called when the person who commits a crime blames the victim for their actions, rather than take responsibility for these actions themselves."

He liked that term for what Edwards was doing. And the jury would view her entire opening statement through that lens.

"We've all experienced it," he continued. "Some of us, most of us maybe, have also done it. We say things like, 'They started it'. 'They made me do it'. 'They pushed my buttons'. And you're going to hear that in this case too. The defendant, Zoey Addison, murdered her boyfriend, Caleb Hirsch. She shot him six times. In the back. And when I'm done talking. Ms. Edwards is going to stand up and tell you it was all Caleb Hirsch's fault. His fault that six bullets tore through his heart and lungs. His fault he bled to death on his own front porch on an otherwise beautiful sunny morning."

Brunelle took a moment to glance back at Addison, and to a lesser extent Edwards. Edwards was doing exactly what he expected: ignoring him and keeping her gaze fixed on the notes she was dutifully taking of his comments. But Addison was staring at him, her eyes rendered even larger than they were the morning of the murder by the gauntness her face had taken on from her prolonged incarceration. It wasn't so much that he wanted to see what she thought of his opening salvo. It was that he knew the jury was looking at her, and he wanted to know what they were seeing.

"Ms. Addison and Mr. Hirsch had been in an on-again, off-again relationship for some time." Brunelle turned back to the jurors. He was going to have to admit Hirsch's mental health issues, but again, he had the opportunity to frame them in the best possible way for his case. "Throughout their relationship, Mr. Hirsch had struggled with mental health challenges. He didn't hide these from Ms. Addison. Indeed, she knew about them and while they sometimes led to the two of them spending time apart, Ms. Addison went into it with both eyes wide open when she and Mr. Hirsch decided their relationship had reached the point where they were ready to move in together."

A relationship point Brunelle was all too familiar with himself as of late.

"They cared about each other," Brunelle continued. "And they took care of each other. Until they didn't. Mr. Hirsch was committed to his recovery and maintaining his mental health. You're going to hear from his treating psychiatrist, Dr. John Young. And you're going to hear that while there was no real cure for his condition, he was making progress and he was invested in his therapy."

That was probably true. Young was also going to tell them that Caleb's mental health was actually degrading leading up to the murder, but Brunelle didn't want to get into that just then.

"But apparently it wasn't enough. Not for Ms. Addison." Another glance at the defendant, following the eyes of the jurors. "Relationships are living things. They move and change and grow, whether you want them to or not. Sometimes they move in the right direction. Sometimes, moving in with someone shows you more of a person than you actually wanted to see. Sometimes, you want to end the relationship. And sometimes, when it's been on-again, off-again for years, you don't know how to do that. Not for real. Not for good."

Brunelle paused. He didn't look at Addison fully again, but he turned his head slightly as if he was going to, but then thought better of it.

"Sometimes you make the wrong decision," he said. "And sometimes you blame the victim for your wrong decision."

Brunelle took a moment to draw a deep breath and center himself again, physically and mentally.

"Zoey Addison made the wrong decision that fateful morning. She chose violence. She chose murder. And now she's going to blame the victim. But after you've heard all the evidence, you'll know it wasn't Caleb Hirsch's fault that Zoey Addison murdered him. It was hers. And we will ask you to return a verdict of guilty to the charge of murder in the first degree. Thank you."

Brunelle walked crisply back to the prosecution table and sat down. Carlisle gave him a sharp nod and whispered, "Good job."

But there were two sides to every story. Especially this one.

"Now, ladies and gentlemen of the jury," Judge Doyle announced, "please give your attention to Ms. Edwards, who will deliver the opening statement on behalf of the defendant."

CHAPTER 32

Edwards performed the exact same steps as Brunelle—stood up, buttoned suit coat, stepped out from behind her table, took her spot in front of the jury—but they were quicker, almost hurried, as if she couldn't wait to respond to Brunelle. That was exactly what Brunelle would have wanted. If Edwards responded directly to his opening, that would mean she was deviating from her prepared remarks. And that would mean she might make a mistake.

But Edwards had been doing this long enough not to make mistakes.

"Good morning, ladies and gentlemen," she started genially. "I'll get to Mr. Brunelle's allegation of 'victim blaming' in due course. But first," she turned fully back toward her client, "I'd like to tell you a little about Zoey."

Humanizing the client, Brunelle knew. Page one of the defense trial strategy playbook. But he could hardly blame her. Page one of the prosecution playbook was humanizing the victim. Brunelle had started that in his opening and their first witness was going to be Dear Ol' Dad.

"Zoey is twenty-three years old," Edwards continued. "She grew up right here in Seattle, and graduated from Roosevelt High School. She enjoys long walks through Discovery Park and painting watercolors down at Gasworks Park and the Ballard Locks. She's a Seattle girl, through and through, and that means she has a big heart. Too big for her own good, maybe."

Edwards took a moment to nod at her own tease, then continued with her Ode to Zoey.

"She met Caleb when they were still in high school. They knew each other, but didn't date then. It was more like they were friends of friends. Caleb played baseball and was into photography. He was a born-and-raised Seattleite too. So, when they ran into each other a year or two after graduation, they started to hang out. There was a natural attraction, a natural connection, and it wasn't long before they started dating. But it wasn't a quick happily-ever-after situation. Far from it. You see, Zoey's greatest strength was that big heart of hers. And Caleb's greatest weakness was that he needed someone with a big heart. A very big heart."

Another solemn pause. It signaled she was about to talk about something difficult, but important. She was going to provide the details Brunelle had glossed over. He just had to hope he'd dug the trenches around Caleb's mental health deep enough to keep Edwards's details within his narrative.

"Caleb suffered from several mental health conditions," she explained. "As the prosecutor told you, you will hear testimony from Dr. John Young, Caleb's treating psychiatrist at the time of the incident in this case."

Again with 'incident', Brunelle thought. But she could hardly say 'murder', he supposed.

"Dr. Young will tell you that Caleb was diagnosed with

schizophrenia, and specifically what is commonly known as paranoid schizophrenia. He also suffered from several personality disorders that exacerbated the schizophrenia. Zoey would learn about the psychological counseling Caleb had during high school, but she didn't know about the schizophrenia diagnosis. She just had to live with it. But then again, there was that big heart of hers."

The big heart motif, Brunelle noted. It was hard not to. He hoped it would start to grate on the jury as well.

"But big heart or not, there were times when Zoey and Caleb needed to take breaks from each other. Not just for Zoey's mental health, but Caleb's too. And you'll hear from Dr. Young about that too. But love is love, as they say, and Zoey decided that she loved Caleb, all of Caleb, for who he was. She was going to do whatever she could to help him be the best version of himself he could be."

Like shoot him in the back six times, Brunelle considered silently.

"They moved in together," Edwards continued, "which can be stressful for any couple."

That's true, Brunelle had to agree.

"And it was even more so for Zoey and Caleb, as Zoey made a commitment to be there with and for Caleb twenty-four hours a day, seven days a week."

Edwards paused again. She took a deep breath and let out an audible sigh. She seemed sad. Brunelle knew that was as scripted as the rest of her presentation.

"Now, why am I telling you all of this?" she asked rhetorically. "I'm telling you all this so you can have some small sense of the impossible decision Zoey would have to make a few months after they moved in together. After Caleb's mental health started to degrade. After his paranoia started to get the best of him. After he filled their home with handguns. After he started suspecting he was being followed. After he thought the children at the school across the street were really the children of the secret government workers monitoring him. After..."

She looked back one last time at Zoey. Brunelle looked too. Zoey was crying. Silently. Her body shaking and tears streaming down from those huge brown eyes.

That was bad, he knew.

"After he told her before bed that he was going to take care of those kids once and for all." Edwards turned back to the jury. "And after he got up the next morning, picked up one of those handguns and told Zoey he was going to murder all of those innocent children. After he ignored her pleas to stop, to call Dr. Young, to call his parents, to do anything but slaughter a playground full of the most innocent and helpless victims imaginable. After he opened the front door and took the first step toward mass murder. And she was faced with that impossible decision. Not because it was difficult to decide. There was only one possible decision, of course. But because it was so difficult to do.

"She went to the hall table and picked up one of those loaded guns Caleb had hid throughout the house. And she killed the man she loved. She shot him six times. Emptied the clip. She stopped him. She had to. For the sake of those children. She really did have no choice."

Then Edwards pointed at Brunelle and scowled at him. "And the prosecutor has the audacity to describe that as 'victim blaming'."

She turned back to the jury. "That's not victim blaming. That's what the law calls necessity. And it's a complete defense to a charge of murder. What she did wasn't as bad as what she prevented, she didn't cause it, and she had no other choice. So, ladies and gentlemen, at the conclusion of the evidence, I will stand up again and ask you to return the only verdict that will be supported by that evidence: not guilty.

"Thank you."

Edwards returned to her still crying client. The lines were drawn. It was time to lay down the color.

"The State may call its first witness," Judge Doyle pronounced from atop the bench.

Carlisle stood up. "The State calls Gerald Hirsch to the stand."

CHAPTER 33

Gerald Hirsch had been waiting in the hallway during the opening statements. He was the first witness, so he needed to be on site and ready to take the stand when they called him, but as a witness he wasn't allowed to listen to the opening statements, lest he, or any other witness, adjust their testimony to help one side or another.

Carlisle was doing the examination so that she would do something immediately after Brunelle. Otherwise, the jury might get the impression Brunelle was doing everything and Carlisle was just handling a few witnesses here and there. It was important the jurors saw Carlisle as an equal partner in the prosecution since she would be delivering the closing argument. And since Carlisle would be doing the examination, it was Brunelle's job to fetch Gerald Hirsch from the hallway.

"We're ready for you, Mr. Hirsch," he said to the elder Hirsch, who was seated on a bench immediately outside the courtroom door. He looked about the same as when they had met with him all those weeks earlier, only sadder. Brunelle had been possibly a dad for all of two hours. He could only imagine what it did to a person who had lost their child. Whose child had been murdered.

Hirsch slipped past Brunelle and made his way to the front of the courtroom. He looked a bit lost, but Brunelle followed close behind and directed him to walk up to the judge's bench for the judge to swear him in. He raised his right hand, swore to tell the truth, the whole truth, and nothing but the truth, and took his seat on the witness stand.

Carlisle waited a moment for Hirsch to get comfortable, but after that moment and a few more, he still didn't look comfortable, so she started anyway.

"Could you please state your name for the record?"

Hirsch leaned forward awkwardly. "Gerald Arnold Hirsh."

"Thank you, Mr. Hirsch," Carlisle replied. "And thank you for coming here to testify. I'm sure this isn't easy for you."

Carlisle wasn't saying all that because she particularly wanted to console Gerald Hirsch, Brunelle knew. But it would look like that to the jury.

"Did you know someone named Caleb Hirsch?" Carlisle continued.

"Did I know him?" Hirsch repeated the question back, somewhat incredulously. "Yes. He was my son."

Carlisle nodded. "Thank you, Mr. Hirsch."

The jury needed to see two types of photographs of a murder victim. Photos that showed the victim was an actual living, breathing human being at some point, and photos that showed that the victim was murdered at some point after that. You didn't use the dad to introduce the second set of photos. Carlisle picked up a single photograph of Caleb while he was still alive from the pile of exhibits on the counter in front of the clerk and walked over to hand it to Gerald Hirsch.

"For the record, I'm handing you what has previously been marked as State's Exhibit 1," she said. "Is this a photo of Caleb?"

Hirsch took the photo from Carlisle and stared at it. Just stared at it. He didn't answer Carlisle's question. She gave him a moment. Then another. Then several more. It was getting uncomfortable.

"Mr. Hirsch?" she interrupted his thoughts.

"Hm?" He finally looked up. "Yes?"

"Is that Caleb?" Carlisle repeated.

He looked down at the photograph again and smiled the saddest smile Brunelle had ever seen. "Yes. That's my Caleb."

That would have been an emotionally powerful place to end the direct examination, but they needed more information from Mr. Hirsch about his Caleb.

"Can we talk a little about some of Caleb's," Carlisle chose her next word carefully, "challenges?"

"You mean his mental illness?" Hirsch got right to it. "Yes. I expected to be asked about that."

Carlisle smiled slightly. She seemed to appreciate being able to get right to it.

"When did Caleb start exhibiting concerning behaviors?" she asked.

Hirsch knew the entire time line like the back of his hand. "Looking back, there were signs even before kindergarten, but it started to become clear when he started puberty. By seventh grade, he was seeing a school counselor. By ninth grade he'd been diagnosed and was seeing a clinical psychologist."

"What was his diagnosis?" Carlisle asked.

Brunelle braced for an objection from Edwards. Hirsch

telling the jury what the doctors had told him was technically hearsay. Edwards could probably block it and require that information to come in only through Young. But she wanted the jury to hear it, so no objection was forthcoming.

"Possible schizophrenic indicators," Hirsch answered, "paranoid personality disorder, and borderline personality disorder."

"That's a lot," Carlisle remarked.

"Yes," Hirsch agreed. "It was."

"What did you do to help him?"

"Like I said, we got him into counseling as soon as it started to present itself," Hirsch answered. "The doctors said we were lucky, that it wasn't very severe, but we didn't feel very lucky."

"I can imagine," Carlisle replied. "Did he continue to see therapists after he graduated from high school?"

Hirsch nodded. "Yes, although then I started to be less involved. He was an adult. He needed to take care of it himself. I don't mean I wasn't willing to help him. The doctors, they told me it was important that he be invested and responsible for his own mental well-being."

"So, what role did you play?"

Hirsch considered the question, then shrugged and looked up earnestly at Carlisle. "I was his dad."

Even Carlisle had to take a moment to allow that answer to dissipate before she continued.

"No further questions, Your Honor," she announced. A good trial attorney knew what to say. A better trial attorney knew when to stop saying it.

"Any cross-examination, Ms. Edwards?" Judge Doyle invited.

"Just briefly, Your Honor," Edwards answered as she stood.

Brunelle wondered if it would really be that brief, but he suspected it probably would be. Hirsch came across as very sympathetic. Edwards wouldn't score any points with the jury by attacking him.

"First of all, let me say I'm very sorry for your loss," she began.

But Hirsch shook his head. "No, I won't let you say that. Your client murdered my son. Don't act like you're not trying to help her get away with murder."

That sent a pulse through the courtroom. Brunelle was surprised, but not as much as Edwards obviously was.

"Um, okay," she stammered. It wasn't like she could get into an argument with him in front of the jury. But she could hardly not ask any questions either and return to her seat with her tail between her legs.

"When was the last time you saw your son?" she tried.

"When I had to identify the body at the morgue," Hirsch answered coldly.

Brunelle was enjoying watching Edwards struggle, but he had to stifle a smile. At any given moment, any one of those jurors might be looking at him. He couldn't look anything other than professional and committed to Truth, Justice, and The American Way.

Edwards's mouth tightened into a thin line. He wasn't going to help her. She was just looking for an exit strategy.

"I mean before he died," Edwards clarified.

"You mean before he was murdered?" Hirsch challenged.

"Fine," Edwards allowed. "When was the last time you saw him before that?"

"I was supposed to have lunch with him that week," Hirsch answered. Or rather didn't quite answer. "But I never got the chance to see him again. I never got the chance to say goodbye."

Edwards rubbed the bridge of her nose for a moment, clearly weighing her options. Then she lowered her hand again and nodded up to the judge. "No further questions, Your Honor."

Hirsch had won that battle handily. And Carlisle was savvy enough not to step on his victory.

"Any redirect examination, Ms. Carlisle?" Judge Doyle inquired.

"No, Your Honor," she answered.

"May this witness be excused?" the judge asked.

Doyle wasn't asking whether Hirsch could leave and go get himself a cup of coffee. A witness being 'excused' was a term of art. It meant they were excused from any further obligation to testify under the subpoena that secured their presence at the trial. An 'excused' witness then became like any other member of the public, which meant they could stay and listen to the testimony of the other witnesses. But as much as Brunelle would have liked to offer that to the father of a murder victim, there was a chance they might need him to testify again at the end of the trial. They wouldn't know whether Addison would testify until she actually took the stand, and if she said something about Caleb that Gerald Hirsch could rebut, then they would need to recall him as a rebuttal witness. Which meant, for the sake of the case, he couldn't be excused.

"No, Your Honor," Carlisle answered. "The State would ask the Court to keep the witness subject to recall."

One party making that request, there was no need to bother asking the other. "Thank you, Mr. Hirsch. You may leave now, but you are subject to being recalled as a witness later in the trial. Please exit the courtroom and wait further instructions from the attorneys."

Hirsch didn't seem to know to be disappointed. He acknowledged the judge's instructions, stood up, and made his way out of the courtroom.

Once he was in the hallway, Judge Doyle looked down at the prosecution table. "The State may call its next witness."

It was Brunelle's turn to stand and announce the witness. "The State calls Detective Larry Chen to the stand."

CHAPTER 34

Chen's entrance was the opposite of Gerald Hirsh's. The detective marched into the courtroom, confident in the procedure ahead. He stopped smartly in front of the judge, raised his right, took the oath, and sat on the witness stand like someone who had done the exact same thing hundreds of times before but still took his responsibility as seriously as the first time he testified.

Brunelle took up a position in the well of the courtroom that allowed all of the jurors to see Chen and enabled Chen to deliver his answers to the jurors without having to look back and forth between them and Brunelle like he was watching a tennis match.

"Please state your name for the record," Brunelle began. That was always the first question.

"Larry Chen."

"How are you employed, sir?" That was always the second question, at least for the professional witnesses like cops.

"I'm a detective with the Seattle Police Department," Chen told the jurors. He was dressed in standard 'detective testifying at trial' regalia. Blazer and slacks, but not a suit. Out of date tie. Badge on his hip.

Brunelle then took him through his experience and duties. Years on the force. Years as a detective. Years doing homicides. By the time they were finished, everyone in the courtroom knew he was an experienced homicide detective. It wasn't like Edwards was contesting that anyway.

"Now I'd like to direct your attention to the homicide in this case," Brunelle moved to the case at bar. "How did you come to be involved in the case?"

"I was the on-call homicide detective that day," Chen explained. "Once it was established that it was in fact a homicide, then I received the call and self-dispatched to the scene."

"How long did it take to establish that it was a homicide?" Brunelle asked.

"Not long, as I recall," Chen answered. "It came in as a homicide call. We just needed to have an officer on scene verify it wasn't a false or inaccurate report."

"Was it either of those things?"

Chen shook his head. "It was not."

"Okay," Brunelle said. "Could you please describe to the jury what you saw when you arrived."

Chen was going to be the witness who Brunelle used to introduce that second set of photos of the victim—the ones that showed he was murdered. Brunelle fetched a stack of photos from in front of the clerk as Chen described the scene to the jurors.

"The residence was a one-story single-family house," he said. "I parked my car on the street and made my way up the front walk. As I approached the porch, I observed an adult male lying face down across the threshold in the doorway. The body was approximately half in and half out of the house, with the head outside on the porch and the feet inside the residence. There was a large amount of blood that had collected under the body both inside the home and on the porch."

"Was it fairly obvious that he was dead?" Brunelle asked.

"It's never possible to confirm only from visual observation," Chen cautioned, "but to the extent it ever is, this was the case."

"Why?"

"Well, as I said, he was face down," Chen answered, "and he had been shot multiple times in the back. I could see the bullet holes in his clothing with the attendant blood stains. Six bullet holes and a pool of blood running off the edge of the porch. I've been doing this long enough to know when to call for the hearse instead of the ambulance."

Brunelle then went through the photos one by one with Chen. He identified the photo, Brunelle moved to admit it, then Chen explained to the jurors what they were seeing, although it wasn't that difficult to understand. When that was done, it was time to move on to the next stage of the investigation.

"So, what did you do next?"

"At any homicide scene, there are two initial objectives," Chen answered. "Secure the integrity of the scene, and locate the suspect. Luckily we were able to do both of those immediately."

"How so?"

"I directed the patrol officers on scene to lock the scene down," Chen answered, "and the suspect was sitting at the kitchen table."

The jury seemed to like that little reveal. Brunelle kept going.

"Who was the suspect?" he asked.

Chen pointed at the defendant. "Zoey Addison."

"And why was she the suspect?"

"Because she told us she killed him."

That was a pretty good reason, Brunelle thought to himself. The jurors were probably thinking that too.

Arguably, Brunelle could have stopped his questioning right there. He had elicited the bare minimum of Addison's confession, and done it in a way that didn't really require the specifics of her statement to be admitted as well. He could finish without the jury hearing the story about the school kids and big hearts and impossible decisions. But the truth was, the jury had already heard all of that in Edwards's opening statement, and they were almost certainly going to hear it when Addison testified, which, while not guaranteed, seemed extremely likely. If Brunelle fought to keep out half of Addison's statement, Edwards would join that battle and the jury would see how hard he was fighting, and conclude it was damaging, maybe even fatal, to his case. That was the fighter's way to try to the case. He wanted to do it the winner's way. It was time to draw the sting again.

"Did you question Ms. Addison about what had happened?" Brunelle asked Chen, as if he hadn't been there himself.

"I did," Chen answered, in the same way.

"What did Ms. Addison tell you?"

So, Chen turned to the jury and recounted what Zoey Addison had told him. Brunelle was impressed by how well Chen remembered the details. He had recorded it, of course, and written a report about it as well, but he was able to recount the conversation almost verbatim from memory. Brunelle supposed that was how you made homicide detective.

Chen went through it all. How she initially asked if he was going to be all right despite being very much not all right, thanks to her. Her description of their relationship and Caleb's mental health problems. Brunelle was sure to bring out that she initially told Chen that Caleb wasn't seeing a therapist, contrary to what Edwards had suggested in her opening statement.

As Chen continued to recount the interrogation, Brunelle was struck by just how much of it centered on Caleb's mental health and the lead-up to the killing. He probably would have lost that argument to keep all of that out after all, since it made up 90 percent of what she said.

Chen reached the end of Addison's statement. The actual shooting.

"Ms. Addison said that she screamed at him to stop," Chen told the jurors, "but that he ignored her. He put on his shoes and unlocked the door. She said she saw one of their guns on the table by the door so she picked it up. She pointed it at him and told him to stop or she would shoot him."

"Did he stop?" Brunelle prompted, even though everyone knew the answer.

"She said he looked at her, but he didn't seem to think she would really shoot him. She told him to stop again and suggested they call a doctor. She said he didn't respond to that suggestion. He just shook his head and opened the door. She told him one more time to stop, but he racked the slide on his gun, loading a bullet into the chamber."

"What did she do next?"

"She said she didn't have any choice."

"Then what?"

"Then she shot him and killed him."

Brunelle nodded. Addison's defense was to the jury after all, but he was able to end on the part that really mattered. She shot him. She killed him. "No further questions, Your Honor."

Edwards stood even as Judge Doyle asked her, "Any cross-examination, counsel?"

"Yes, Your Honor," Edwards answered.

Even if Brunelle had brought everything out, she couldn't be seen not cross-examining the lead detective. Brunelle was curious where she would go with him, although he had his suspicions.

"You've been a detective for over twenty years, is that right, Detective Chen?" she began.

"That's correct," Chen confirmed.

"And more than ten years as a homicide detective, is that right?"

"Yes," Chen answered.

"Very impressive."

Chen just shrugged. There wasn't really a question to respond to.

"So, you're familiar with the elements of the crime of murder?" she asked.

"I am," Chen confirmed.

"And you would also be familiar with the defenses to a charge of murder," Edwards put to him. "Correct?"

"That is correct," Chen answered.

"Insanity? Diminished capacity? Self-defense?" Edwards listed a few.

"Yes, yes, and yes," Chen answered.

"What about necessity?" Edwards asked. "Are you familiar with the legal defense of necessity?"

Chen nodded slowly. "I am."

"I'm going to object at this point." Brunelle stood to address the Court. "Legal arguments are for closing arguments, not witness examination. It would not be appropriate to ask this witness, or any witness, whether they believe the elements of the crime or the elements of a given defense have been established."

Judge Doyle frowned along to Brunelle's objection, then looked down at Edwards. "Is that what you were going to do?"

"No, Your Honor," Edwards answered. "I'm not going to ask Detective Chen whether he thinks that the defense of necessity has been established. I am going to ask him about certain facts and I may argue later that those facts establish the defense. But nothing more than that."

Doyle nodded a few more times as he considered the objection and the response. "I'm going to overrule the objection. You may proceed, Ms. Edwards."

Edwards thanked the judge, then extracted a single sheet of paper from a file on the defense table. No one else in the courtroom could read it, but everyone knew by then that it was a list of the elements of the necessity defense.

"Ms. Addison told you that she believed she had to shoot Mr. Hirsch in order to prevent him from murdering schoolchildren, didn't she?"

Chen nodded. "She said that, yes."

"Ms. Addison told you that she believed Mr. Hirsch would kill far more than just one child, didn't she?"

Chen twisted his mouth in thought. "I'm not sure she said that explicitly, but that seemed to be the assumption, yes."

Edwards was actually checking off the elements on her paper, and performatively so, to make sure no one overlooked what she was doing.

"Ms. Addison told you that it was Mr. Hirsch who threatened to kill those children, correct? It wasn't her idea, right?"

"She said it was his idea," Chen confirmed.

"And finally," Edwards said, "she said she tried to get him to call a doctor rather than go through with his plan but he refused, correct?"

"That's what she told us, yes," Chen confirmed.

Edwards started to check off that last element of necessity, then stopped herself dramatically and asked Chen another question. "If she had called 911, it would have taken several minutes for law enforcement to respond, isn't that correct?"

Chen tried to wriggle off the hook. "Response times vary."

Edwards dropped her head to one side and grinned slightly at him. She had the advantage that she knew Chen would tell the truth, even if it hurt the prosecution.

"Detective Chen," she took a step toward him, "you've been a detective for over twenty years. You know how quickly officers can respond, even the most righteous and heroic officers. If Zoey had let Caleb walk out that door and called 911, even if they responded the fastest they had ever responded to any call, law enforcement would not have arrived in time to stop Caleb, would they have?"

Brunelle could have objected because the question called for speculation. But Doyle would have overruled it and then it would have hurt twice as much when Chen answered.

"No," he admitted. "I don't believe they would have responded in time to stop him."

Edwards made a show of placing her final checkmark on her paper, then declared, "No further questions."

Brunelle couldn't let it end on that.

"Any redirect-examination, Mr. Brunelle?" the judge asked.

Brunelle stood up. "Yes, Your Honor."

He came out from behind the table just enough to ask two questions.

"You know the elements of the defense of necessity, correct, Detective Chen?"

"Yes, I do," he answered.

"And being fully aware and well-versed in that defense," Brunelle asked, "after hearing Ms. Addison's story, you still went ahead and arrested her, didn't you?"

"Yes, I did."

"No further questions," Brunelle announced.

It wasn't a win, but he'd take the draw. There was a lot of trial ahead.

CHAPTER 35

Chen was followed by a series of patrol officers and forensic technicians. It wasn't so much that they had important evidence to impart to the jury as it was that if a particular cop involved in the case didn't testify, Edwards could claim Brunelle and Carlisle had elected not to call them because they would have said something damaging to the State's case. That was always a concern in any case, but it was a heightened concern when there was, by all accounts, a potentially important piece of evidence that had not been recovered. If Officer Smith or Technician Jones didn't testify, then Edwards would claim they were the one who absconded with the holy grail journal while Chen's back was turned.

The fact that Edwards wasn't contesting identity or causality made the examinations go more quickly than they might otherwise have. No questions about other possible suspects, or the feasibility of potential alibis, or alternative causes of death. Even the testimony of the Medical Examiner, usually a point of high drama in a murder case, lacked its usual energy.

"Were you able to determine a cause of death, Dr.

Jacoby?"

"Yes, I was."

"And what was the cause of death?"

"Multiple gunshot wounds to the posterior torso, resulting in the laceration of multiple vital organs and uncontrolled internal bleeding."

"Were you able to determine a manner of death, Dr. Jacoby?"

"Yes, I was."

"What was the manner of death?"

"Homicide!"

Yawn.

Edwards's cross-examination was short and direct.

"Your autopsy didn't tell you *why* my client shot the victim six times in the back, did it?"

"No, it did not."

"No further questions."

When, after days and weeks of trial, all but one of the State's witnesses had testified, the who, what, when, and where of the murder had all been established beyond any doubt, reasonable or otherwise. They saved the why for last.

"The State calls Dr. John Young to the stand."

CHAPTER 36

Young's testimony fell on an afternoon. That seemed right somehow. Brunelle and Carlisle knew they were going to rest after he was finished testifying. Edwards could deduce that too. Brunelle wasn't sure about Judge Doyle, but he suspected the jury could feel the energy of the State's case-in-chief culminating with the psychiatrist who treated the victim whose mental health problems were the crux of the entire case.

Young dressed up for trial, even more than he had for the motion hearing. Dark suit, white shirt, no tie. Brunelle thought he had a fresh haircut too. His teeth looked even brighter too. Brunelle supposed it probably wasn't every day the doctor got to be the star witness for the prosecution.

Brunelle really hoped it would be for the prosecution.

"Do you swear or affirm that you will tell the truth, the whole truth, and nothing but the truth?"

"I do," Young declared almost a little too loudly.

He walked crisply to the witness stand, sat down smoothly, and leaned forward, ready for Brunelle's first question.

It was always the same first question. "Please state your

name for the record."

"John Logan Young," he replied with a serious expression that Brunelle found both totally appropriate for the circumstances and also somehow less than genuine.

Brunelle hoped the impression was simply caused by his own desire to be finished with the trial and not something more that the jury might also sense.

"How are you employed, sir?" Brunelle continued.

"I am a clinical psychiatrist," Young answered. "I am self-employed and own my own practice."

Brunelle then took him through his education and experience again. The degrees and the residencies. The years of experience. The expertise only all of that education and expertise could provide. Then it was time to talk about the case.

"Were you acquainted with a young man by the name of Caleb Hirsch?"

"Yes, I was," Young confirmed.

"How were you acquainted with him?"

"He was one of my patients."

"How long was he a patient of yours?" Brunelle continued to lay the foundation. That's what direct examination was all about, even if it seemed silly to non-lawyers sometimes.

"Caleb came to me about six months ago," Young answered.

"And how long was he a patient?" Brunelle had to repeat the actual question, even if just to get the answer in the record.

"Until his death," Young said it out loud.

Brunelle nodded. He could move along. "What were you treating Caleb for?"

Young also nodded, but not the checklist nod of a prosecutor asking non-leading questions. It was the nod of a thoughtful professional about to impart important insights.

"Caleb was a very troubled young man," Young began.

Brunelle sighed internally. He didn't need Young to make himself seem important by playing up Caleb's pathology.

"I was able to diagnose Caleb as suffering from the onset of schizophrenia, paranoid type. He also had the traits of several attendant personality disorders, although not all of them rose to the level of a diagnosable disorder."

"That sounds like a lot," Brunelle went ahead and said it. The jury was thinking it anyway. And people who wanted to seem smart were quick to show their superior knowledge by disagreeing, which is what Brunelle actually wanted him to do.

"Well, I'm not sure I would say that," Young responded. "All of us have our own demons, so to speak. Any one of us could probably be seen to exhibit at least some of the criteria of a mental illness, especially a personality disorder. In most people, those behaviors don't rise to the level of a diagnosis, but they aren't completely absent either."

Like narcissistic personality disorder, Brunelle thought regarding his witness.

"So, yes, Caleb had his issues," Young continued, "but we all do. And he was working on them." He placed a fist to his heart. "*We* were working on them. Together."

"I'm glad to hear that," Brunelle said. And he was. Mostly on a professional level. On a personal level, it hadn't worked out for Caleb after all. "What exactly were you and Caleb doing to address his mental health challenges?"

Young launched into a jargon-filled explanation of the treatments and therapies he had tried with Caleb. The primary one was drugs, at least for the schizophrenia.

"Caleb presented a challenge," Young explained.

"Schizophrenia is usually best treated with pharmaceuticals. So-called talk therapy is usually of minimal value. The personality disorders, on the other hand, require the sort of behavior modification therapies that are ineffective against most forms of schizophrenia. We made the decision to tackle the schizophrenia first, largely because we wouldn't be able to make progress on the other issues if that weren't brought to a manageable level."

"Were you able to do that?" Brunelle asked.

"I think so," Young answered.

That was Brunelle's best hope for a successful direct examination of Young: the fact that the doctor wanted to think he'd done a good job, and would want to tell the jury that. He certainly didn't seem like he thought he'd done a bad job.

"It can be difficult to assess, and things can change," Young qualified his answer, "but I believed we had it under control prior to, well, prior to his death."

Brunelle stifled a frown. He didn't like his star witness avoiding the word 'murder'.

"And that allowed you the space to work on the other issues?" Brunelle asked.

"Well, it would have," Young answered, "but we didn't get the chance because of what happened."

Fine, Brunelle would say it. "Because of his murder?"

"Yes," Young agreed.

Brunelle took a moment to gather his thoughts for the next area of inquiry. He rubbed a hand over his mouth and took a deep breath. He didn't feel completely confident as to exactly what Young would say, but he couldn't not ask the questions either.

"There has been testimony in the trial," Brunelle began, "that Caleb was becoming increasingly paranoid in the days leading up to his murder. That he believed he was being followed and monitored. And, most importantly to this case, that he believed the students at the elementary school up the street from his house were actually the children of those actors who were monitoring him, that they were in on it. Did you and Caleb ever talk about any such delusions?"

Young nodded solemnly. "We did."

Brunelle could hardly avoid that. But he could show the jury that Caleb's thoughts about the children did not extend to murder.

"What did he say about the children?"

"He indicated a belief," Young explained, "that they were the children of the adults who were monitoring him."

"At any time, did he indicate a desire to hurt those children?"

"No, he did not," Young gave him.

That was huge. Brunelle relaxed somewhat. But he wasn't quite done yet. One last sting to draw.

"As part of your therapy with Caleb," he asked, "did you ask him to keep a journal of his thoughts?"

Young nodded. "I did, yes."

"And did he do that?"

"Yes, although with varying degrees of consistency," Young answered.

"Was he supposed to share those journals with you?" Brunelle asked. "Or was it more of a private diary?"

"A little bit of both, I would say," Young answered, predictably. "They were supposed to be his honest, private thoughts. But part of therapy is sharing those honest private thoughts with your therapist. So, yes it was a private diary, but also yes, he was supposed to share it with me."

"Did he share it with you?"

Young nodded. "Yes. We would often go over journal entries in our sessions, as was appropriate."

Brunelle winced slightly. "So, not every session? And not every entry?"

Young shrugged. "There are only so many minutes in a session, and only so many sessions in a month. I had to focus on whatever was most pressing at that particular session. Sometimes, that involved reviewing his journal entries. Sometimes it didn't."

"How long before his death," Brunelle started, but then caught himself doing it too, "before his *murder*, was the last time you saw Caleb?"

"Ten days," Young answered. "I checked my records. We were meeting every other week, and we had an appointment scheduled four days after his, his murder."

"At that last session before his murder," Brunelle was almost done, "did you review his journal?"

Young frowned. "I checked my clinical notes before coming here today and I didn't make any notations about reviewing his journal."

"Do you recall even seeing it then?" Brunelle asked. "Did he bring it with him?"

"He may have brought it," Young asked, "but if I didn't ask to see it, it might have stayed in his backpack the entire time."

"And do you know where the journal is today?"

Young shook his head. "It's my understanding that the police never found it. But I certainly didn't have it. There would be no point to the journal if I kept it at my office and he could only access it every fourteen days."

Homestretch. Young had done well. Brunelle needed to wrap it up. Of course, Edwards would get her chance then, but he couldn't do anything about that.

"So, in summary," Brunelle asked, "Caleb never mentioned in any of your sessions, or from what you saw in his journal, any desire to murder the school children across the street from his house, or anywhere else for that matter?"

Young took a moment. He obviously knew his answer was important. That was why he'd worn the suit. "I have no personal recollection or any clinical notes indicating that he mentioned a desire to harm the children at that school or any other."

Good answer. "Thank you, Doctor. No further questions."

Brunelle returned to his seat next to Carlisle. "I'm not sure that could have gone better," she remarked in a whisper. Brunelle nodded. He thought so too, but it was Edwards's turn to manipulate the doctor's narcissism to say what she wanted.

"Do you feel any responsibility for Caleb's death?" Edwards started.

Or she might just attack him, Brunelle considered.

"I wish I could have helped him more," Young answered, "but I'm not the one who pulled the trigger. So, no, I don't feel responsible for his death, his murder." He wasn't going to shy away from that word after Edwards came at him like that.

"Doesn't successful therapy," Edwards continued, "often involve building supports with a patient's family to help them follow up and follow through with the treatments they need to get better and stay better?"

"That is often the case, yes," Young agreed. "Those sort of supports can be vital."

"So, why didn't you do that for Caleb?"

Young's expression became confused. He tipped his head slightly. "I believe I did."

"My client didn't know Caleb was seeing you," Edwards pointed out.

"Ah." Young nodded. "Yes. Well, you see, patient confidentiality prevents me from reaching out to just anyone who might be helpful and telling them about a patient's diagnoses and treatment plans. I was working with Caleb's father, but the reason Ms. Addison didn't know Caleb was seeing me was because Caleb didn't want her to know."

Edwards crossed her arms. "Why not?"

"Well, I suppose you'd need to ask him to know for sure," Young answered, "but of course we can't do that now. But, my clinical opinion, based on what he said in our sessions, is that he was embarrassed. He didn't want Ms. Addison to know he was in therapy again because he was afraid she would break it off again. Those fears were part of the pathology, I'm afraid."

Brunelle wasn't sure if that information helped or hurt him. But it seemed to surprise Edwards a bit, which he knew was good for him.

"You said you have no recollection of Mr. Hirsch mentioning anything to you about hurting those school kids, is that right?" she asked. "No paranoid delusions or homicidal ideations?"

"No, nothing like that," Young agreed.

"But just because he didn't mention them to you," Edwards followed up, "doesn't mean he wasn't experiencing them, does it?"

Young frowned. "I'd like to say that my patients always tell me everything, and I try to establish relationships where they feel safe to do so, but I have to agree with you. Just because a patient doesn't share something with me doesn't mean they aren't experiencing it."

"And so to be crystal clear," Edwards pressed, "just because Caleb Hirsch didn't tell you he wanted to murder school children doesn't mean he didn't want to do that."

"Correct," Young answered.

"And his journal is lost," Edwards pointed out.

"Yes," Young agreed.

"So, if we wanted to know whether he was actually thinking that terrible, horrific thing," Edwards put to him, "then we would have to look elsewhere, to other statements he may have made to other people, correct?"

"That makes sense," Young allowed.

"Other people like his girlfriend, Zoey Addison, right?" Edwards asked.

Young grinned at the advocacy. "Sure."

"No further questions, Your Honor." Edwards returned to her seat next to her client, who likely offered her words of encouragement similar to those Carlisle gave Brunelle.

"Any redirect examination, Mr. Brunelle?" Judge Doyle asked.

Brunelle rose to his feet to answer. On the one hand, Edwards had done some damage. On the other hand, the points she raised were true, so it was unlikely Young could or would do much to blunt them. Sometimes it was best to leave the arguments for closing arguments.

"No, Your Honor."

Young was excused and Judge Doyle looked to the prosecutors. "Does the State have any further witnesses?"

"No, Your Honor," Brunelle, still standing, answered. "The State rests."

CHAPTER 37

The time immediately after the State rested its case was called 'halftime', even though the defense case was usually considerably shorter than the prosecution's. Sometimes the defense didn't put on any evidence at all, so 'halftime' was followed immediately by closing arguments. Brunelle allowed himself to hope Edwards might not put Addison on the stand, afraid, as any good defense attorney should be, of exposing her client to cross-examination by the prosecutor. For one thing, such a decision would mean less work for Brunelle and a sooner end to the trial. For another, it would make Edwards's argument for an acquittal on the necessity defense a much harder sell if Addison didn't tell the jury herself that she had no choice but to kill the love of her life heroically in order to save a schoolyard full of innocent children.

And that was the exact reason Edwards called her client to the stand when the case reconvened the next morning.

"The defense," she announced proudly when prompted by the judge, "calls Zoey Addison to the stand."

Addison stepped out from the defense table for the first

time in the entire trial. All eyes were on her as she walked first to the judge's bench to be sworn in, then to the witness stand, to give her testimony. She was dressed in a navy suit with a cream shell underneath, dark stockings and flats. Edwards had managed to gather together four different outfits for her to wear during the course of the trial, so the jury had seen each of them by then, several times over. The same was true for Brunelle's suits, however. And Carlisle's and Edwards's. It had been a long trial. But they were almost done. Edwards didn't have any other witnesses. Addison would be the last.

Despite the formal attire, on the witness stand Addison looked even younger, even more frightened than she had the morning of the murder. Those big brown eyes were fixed on Edwards as she slowly made her way to the center of the well and began her examination.

"Could you please state your full name for the record?"

"Zoey Claire Addison," she answered, her voice cracking a bit on the first syllable she'd said in open court since the case began.

"You are the defendant in this case, are you not?" Edwards had to ask the same silly questions on direct exam that Brunelle and Carlisle had had to.

"Yes, I am," Addison confirmed.

There was no need to go through her education and experience. Unless she had experience shooting people in the back. Brunelle certainly would have liked to have heard that, but just as certainly, Edwards wouldn't have asked about it.

"Did you know Caleb Hirsh?"

Addison froze at the name. She blinked hard and her eyes began to glisten. Brunelle had to fight to keep from shaking his head.

"Yes," she croaked.

"How did you know him?" Edwards wasn't about to give her a chance to compose herself. The best thing Addison could do for her defense was to break down at the thought of her lost love.

But Addison managed to put on a stiff upper lip and answer the question without sobbing. "He was my boyfriend."

Then it was time for the recitation that did matter: the recitation of their relationship. It was pretty much what she had told Chen the morning of the murder and what Edwards had told the jury in her opening statement. They sort of knew each other in high school but not really. They ran into each other years later, matching on a dating app. They went out for coffee. Then dinner. Then this really cool speakeasy hidden in the basement of an otherwise unused building on the edge of Capitol Hill. They hit it off and started dating in earnest. It was good, until it wasn't.

"What caused you to break up the first time?" Edwards asked.

"I didn't realize it at the time," Addison explained, "but it was his mental health issues. I thought he was just really emotional and it got harder and harder to be around him. I felt like I was walking on eggshells and I guess I just decided that I was too young to start living my life like that, so I broke it off."

"Did you get back together with Caleb?"

"Yes."

"About how long after that first break-up?"

"About six months, I think," Addison answered. "Maybe a little more."

"And why did you agree to start seeing him again?"

"Because he told me the truth," Addison answered, visibly happy by the memory. "He told me about his past mental health issues. He told me that he really liked me and he wanted to spend time with me. I really liked him too, and wanted to spend time with him. At least, the way he was when we first started dating."

"How long did that second round of the relationship last?" Edwards asked.

Addison hesitated. "It's kind of hard to say exactly. There were some bumps in the road. There were good days and bad days. I had to establish boundaries to keep myself emotionally safe. When Caleb crossed one of those boundaries, we took a break until I could feel safe again. That went on for a while, but eventually he learned I was serious about my boundaries and he learned how to not cross them."

"Is that when you decided to move in together?" Edwards continued.

"Yes," Addison confirmed. "It took a while to find a place we could afford, but then we ran across this sweet little house for rent in this really quiet neighborhood. It was perfect, so we applied and a bit to our surprise, we got it."

"Why to your surprise?" Edwards wondered.

Addison shrugged. "I don't know. It's just that when things don't always go the way you want them to, you start getting used to that, so you're surprised when something good happens."

Brunelle could relate to that. He supposed most of the jurors could too.

"Was Caleb still in therapy at that point?"

Addison frowned. A deep frown that pulled her mouth not just down, but in somehow. "I didn't think so. He told me he had finished therapy."

"But that wasn't accurate, was it?" Edwards prompted.

"I guess it wasn't," Addison answered. "I learned through

all the stuff with this case that he was secretly seeing that Dr. Young."

"He didn't tell you?"

"No."

"Why not?"

"Objection!" Brunelle interjected. He would be doing the cross-examination—it was his case, after all—so he had to be the one to make objections, not Carlisle. "Calls for speculation."

It did, so Edwards didn't have a reply ready.

"I'll sustain the objection," Judge Doyle ruled. "Please ask your next question, Ms. Edwards."

Edwards nodded at the judge and did just that. Except it was the same question, phrased in a way that Brunelle couldn't object.

"Would it have bothered you to know Caleb was back in therapy?"

Addison took a moment and sighed before answering. "I don't know. I wanted him to be cured, you know? I mean, I knew he would never be one hundred percent cured. That's not how mental health works. But I wanted him to find a place of equilibrium. It seemed like he had. That's why I thought we could move in together."

"So, if you had known he was seeing a therapist again," Edwards posited, "you might not have agreed to move in together?"

Brunelle knew there was a joke there about him telling Casey he was seeing a psychiatrist to avoid moving in together, but he ignored it to stay focused on the testimony.

"Yeah, I guess," Addison answered. "Maybe. I'm not sure. But I wish I could have been able to make that choice myself."

"After you moved in together," Edwards moved along, "did you start to see any indications that his mental health was declining again?"

"Yeah," Addison nodded somberly. "I tried to ignore the signs at first, but they started getting worse. I actually was thinking he should maybe start seeing someone again. If I'd known he already was and it was still getting worse... well, that would explain why it got so crazy so fast."

"What got crazy fast?" Edwards asked.

"All the paranoid stuff," Addison answered. "Suddenly he started talking about people watching him. I thought he just meant rude people at the bus stop or something, making him feel bad about himself. But then he started talking about being followed. He bought a gun for protection. Then another, and another, and another. He started pulling the curtains closed whenever we were home and he wouldn't use his phone anymore. Our sweet little house started to feel like a prison."

"And you didn't know why," Edwards added.

"I didn't know why," Addison agreed. "And then he started talking about the kids at the school across the street. And that scared me."

"What did he say about the children at the school?" Edwards asked.

Addison shook her head and chuckled darkly at the memory. "He said they weren't really school children. I mean, they were real children, but they didn't really go to school there. They were the children of whatever government or secret organization was watching him. They were in on it. They thought they could fool him. But he knew what they were doing." She sighed again. "It was really bad. The worst I'd ever seen."

"So, what did you do about it?" Edwards asked her client,

if a bit brusquely.

Addison's shoulders dropped and her eyes widened again. "Nothing," she admitted. "I didn't do anything. I should have called his old therapist, or his dad. Somebody. But I didn't. I think I was just so scared it wasn't going to work again. I tried talking to him about it, but he wouldn't talk to me anymore. He wouldn't say anything else about those kids. Not until the night before..." she paused. "The night before I shot him."

At least she admitted to that, Brunelle thought. One less question for cross-examination. Although he'd probably ask it anyway.

"What did he say that night?" Edwards prompted.

"Right before he went to sleep," Addison answered, "he said, 'I've got a solution for those kids tomorrow.' I asked him what he meant, but all he said was that he talked to his dad about it and he had a solution about those kids. Then he just rolled over and wouldn't say another word to me."

That was all new information, Brunelle noted. Addison never said anything to Chen about cryptic threats the night before. And she certainly never said that Caleb had talked to his dad about his delusions. Brunelle was suddenly very glad they had not excused Gerald Hirsh from further testimony.

"We need to—" he started to whisper to Carlisle.

"Get Hirsch back here to testify in rebuttal," Carlisle finished the thought. She pulled out her phone. "I'm on it. Larry will get him here ASAP."

"What happened the next morning?" Edwards continued her examination. Brunelle returned his attention to her. She had finally reached the facts that actually mattered, at least in Brunelle's opinion.

"Everything seemed fine at first," Addison answered. "In

fact, he was happier than I'd seen him for a while. He even let me open the front curtains to let in the morning sun without a fight. I thought maybe things were going to go back to being good again. I hoped that. But..." Addison trailed off and looked away, her eyes swelling with tears again.

"But what?" Edwards asked. "What happened?"

Addison had to take several moments to regain her composure, and even after she managed that, her voice still trembled. "He finished his breakfast, then he stood up and walked over to the small table next to his favorite chair. He opened the drawer, pulled out a gun and said, just as calm and normal as ever, 'I'm going to go kill those children now.'"

Brunelle stole a glance at the jurors. They were either believing Addison completely, or they weren't buying it. He wanted to gauge their reactions. But they had gotten used to sitting stoically over the last several weeks. One man had his arms crossed, usually a sign of disbelief, but he might have been sitting like that all morning, for all Brunelle knew. Brunelle looked back to the defendant.

"What did you do?" Edwards asked, allowing a practiced undertone of panic into her voice.

"I couldn't believe it," Addison answered. "I thought maybe I heard him wrong, so I asked him, 'What did you say?' and he very calmly answered, 'I'm going to kill those children at the school,' then he headed for the front door with the gun in his hand."

"Did you try to stop him?" Edwards asked.

"I followed him and told him to not do it," Addison answered. "I said, 'You can't go kill those school kids. They're just innocent little children.' But he laughed—I remember he laughed because I hadn't seen him laugh in so long—he laughed and said, 'They're not innocent.' Then he sat down and started putting his shoes on."

"What happened next?"

"I begged for him to stop," Addison answered, her voice growing higher and faster. "I told him we could call a doctor. We could call his dad. I told him to just put the gun down and we could figure something out."

"Did that work?"

"No!" Addison sobbed. "He wouldn't listen to me at all. He just grabbed the doorknob and said, 'I'll be right back,' like he was going out to buy milk or something. He wasn't listening to me. He wasn't listening to anything."

"So what did you do?" Edwards asked.

"I saw one of those damned guns sitting on top of the table in the hallway by the door," Addison answered through tears, "so I picked it up and pointed it at him. I told him to stop or I'd shoot him. I begged him to stop. I begged him."

"Did he stop?"

Addison shook her head. "No," she rasped, almost a whisper.

"I'm sorry." Edwards took a half step toward her in encouragement. "I know this is difficult, but I need you to keep your voice up so the jury can hear you. Did he stop?"

"No," Addison answered loudly. "He didn't stop. He opened the door and started walking outside."

"And what did you do?"

Addison didn't answer at first. She looked down at the floor and blinked those big eyes of hers, sending teardrops falling onto the carpet. She started shaking her head to herself, then finally she stopped, looked up again and turned to the jurors. "I shot him."

Edwards let the answer linger for a moment. Then she asked, "How many times?"

"I don't know," Addison answered. The tears had stopped, but she had the same mascara-tinted streaks down her cheeks as the first time Brunelle had met her. "Enough times. Enough times to stop him."

Edwards took a few more moments to allow her client's story to sink in with everyone in the courtroom. Then she just needed to check off that element of the necessity defense: 'no reasonable legal alternative existed.'

"Why didn't you call the police?" she asked.

"There wasn't time." Addison had turned back to face her attorney, but her eyes were staring a thousand yards past Edwards.

"Why didn't you call his dad?"

"There wasn't time."

"Why didn't you do something else? Anything else?"

"There wasn't time," Addison answered. Then her eyes came back into focus and she choked back a sob. "And they were *children*."

That was the perfect place, the perfect response, for Edwards to end her questioning. "No further questions, Your Honor."

Edwards sat down and Brunelle stood up.

"Any cross-examination, Mr. Brunelle?" the judge asked.

The answer had to be, "Yes, Your Honor." Even if Brunelle had nothing to ask her, he couldn't just not challenge the defendant. The jury would acquit in five minutes, and it would only take that long because two of them needed to use the bathroom.

Brunelle stepped out from behind the prosecution table

and took up his own spot in the well of the courtroom. He was about two steps closer to Addison than Edwards had been. Edwards had wanted Addison to feel comfortable. Brunelle wanted her to feel threatened.

"You shot and killed Caleb Hirsch, correct?" he got right to it.

Addison's eyes were wide again, but they weren't teary. They were scared. Of Brunelle. That was probably good, he decided.

"Yes," she answered.

He had just proven his case. The problem was, Edwards had just proven her defense.

"The story you told the jury about Caleb threatening to kill school children," Brunelle asked, "no one else heard any of that, correct?"

"No," Addison admitted. "I mean there was no one else there."

"And the story you just told the jury," Brunelle repeated that turn of phrase, "it was a different story from what you told Detective Chen, wasn't it?"

Addison's brow furrowed. "I don't think so."

"You told the jury just now that Caleb told you he had a solution for the children the night before you shot and killed him," Brunelle recounted, "but you never told Detective Chen anything about Caleb saying something the night before, did you?"

Addison shrugged slightly. "I, I think I did."

Brunelle shook his head. "No, you didn't." Then he asked another question.

"You told the jury just now that Caleb told you he had talked to his dad about this solution for the children," Brunelle said, "but you never told Detective Chen that, did you?"

Again, Addison squirmed slightly in her seat. "I think I probably did. I mean, I meant to, but maybe I forgot. I was in kind of a panic. I had just shot my boyfriend."

"Yes, you had," Brunelle agreed.

He took another half step toward her, just to make sure he was definitely inside her personal space.

"You told the jury just now that the reason you shot and killed Caleb Hirsch was to save the lives of those school children down the street."

"That's right," Addison agreed.

"But isn't it true that you were going to break it off with him again? At least if he kept acting the way he was acting and refused to get help? You had boundaries, right? You weren't going to stay around if he violated your boundaries again, isn't that what you told the jury?"

Addison squirmed again. Her eyes darted around the courtroom. "I mean, yes, probably," she admitted. "I don't know, but yes, I was trying to figure out if I should stay."

"Because if you left," Brunelle explained for her, "it was going to be messy. There was the joint lease agreement to try to get out of. You'd probably already integrated your pots and pans and streaming passwords. And it was the third time—or more, depending on how you count it—that you had gotten together with him. If you left, you had to think maybe there was just going to be a fourth time and a fifth time, right?"

"I don't know." Addison crossed her arms. "I hadn't really thought about it that far."

"It was like you were never going to be able to get away from him," Brunelle continued. "And now instead of a few hours at a trendy little speakeasy on Capitol Hill, you were living in an armed prison, curtains drawn, phones off, guns everywhere. You said it was like a prison. But you can't have a prison without a prison. You were the prisoner. And you wanted out."

"Are you saying that's why I shot Caleb?" Addison shrieked at him. "That I killed Caleb to get away from him, not to save those kids?"

"I'm saying the only way you avoid going from Caleb's prison to a real prison for murder," Brunelle answered, "is if the jury believes the story you told them. I'm saying your story changed. And I'm saying that when you're done testifying, we're going to recall Caleb's dad and Detective Chen to tell the jury that you changed your story, so they know none of it was ever true anyway."

"Objection!" Edwards finally interrupted. "The prosecutor is badgering the witness. He's not even asking any questions at this point."

"No speeches, Mr. Brunelle," the judge admonished. "Ask a question."

But Brunelle didn't have any. "No further questions, Your Honor."

"Any redirect examination, Ms. Edwards?" Judge Doyle asked.

Edwards had a strategic decision to make. If she asked more questions, Brunelle would have the opportunity to recross-examine her client, perhaps doing additional damage. If she didn't ask any more questions, then Addison's testimony would be concluded as a matter of law and she could not be recalled to the witness stand by the State. Did whatever benefit she might gain from trying to rehabilitate her client outweigh the risk of further confrontation with Brunelle?

She sighed and looked up at the judge, her hands balled

into fists. "No further questions, Your Honor."

Judge Doyle nodded and looked down at Addison. "Your testimony is concluded. Please return to your seat next to your attorney."

Once Addison had done so, the judge posed another question to Edwards. "Does the defense have any further witnesses?"

"No, Your Honor," Edwards answered. "The defense rests."

Doyle turned to the prosecution table. Everyone knew the answer to the question he was about to pose—Brunelle had already stated his intentions—but he had to pose it anyway. "Does the State wish to call any rebuttal witnesses?"

"Yes, Your Honor," Brunelle responded. "The State will recall Gerald Hirsch to the stand."

Carlisle stood up and pointed to her phone. "But not for like fifteen minutes, Your Honor. Traffic."

CHAPTER 38

Judge Doyle called a thirty-minute recess to allow enough time for both Gerald Hirsch and Chen to arrive. Chen was on his way too, but he had been out at a scene in West Seattle, so it was going to take him more than fifteen minutes to get over the West Seattle Bridge and back downtown. Brunelle and Carlisle waited impatiently in the hallway, but soon enough Gerald Hirsch walked down the long corridor to the entrance to Judge Doyle's courtroom.

"Thank you for coming back, Mr. Hirsch," Brunelle said when Caleb's father arrived. "We're sorry to do this to you. I'm sure this isn't easy for you."

But Gerald Hirsch just shrugged his tired shoulders. "Caleb was my kid. Parents will do anything for their children. I'll do whatever it takes to hold his killer responsible."

"Thank you," Carlisle repeated Brunelle's sentiment. "It won't take as long as last time. We just have a few very specific questions for you."

"About what?" Hirsch asked, reasonably enough.

But the law was often less than reasonable.

"We can't tell you," Brunelle answered. "That would undermine the purpose of preventing witnesses from hearing each other's testimony. But it'll be clear enough once we get started, I promise."

"Are you going to ask the questions again?" Hirsch asked Carlisle.

Carlisle looked to Brunelle. "Good question." They hadn't settled that yet.

"I'd like to do the questioning this time," Brunelle said. He was happy for Carlisle's help, and it was important for the jury to see an equal partnership, but it was still his case. He wanted to drive it across the finish line. "It's based on some things I elicited, so I think it makes the most sense if I do it."

There was no argument from Carlisle, and Hirsch just shrugged again. The thirty minutes was almost over. Hirsch took a seat on the hallway bench just as they spied Chen rushing down the hallway toward them.

"What's going on?" he asked when he reached them.

"Carlisle will tell you when you get on the stand," Brunelle answered. "We're switching it up for rebuttal."

Chen looked askance at Carlisle but she just smiled. "I'll be gentle."

* * *

"All rise!" the bailiff called out at the end of the recess. "The King County Superior Court is back in session, The Honorable Nathan Doyle presiding."

Everyone save the jury was reassembled. "Are your witnesses here?" Judge Doyle asked the prosecution team.

"Yes, Your Honor," Brunelle answered. "Gerald Hirsch will be first, followed by Detective Chen, and they are both seated in the hallway outside the courtroom."

"Very well," Doyle responded. He directed his bailiff to bring the jury in. The lawyers remained standing while the jurors filed into place. Then Judge Doyle looked again at the prosecution table.

"Please call your first rebuttal witness, Mr. Brunelle," he instructed.

"The State recalls Gerald Hirsch," Brunelle repeated his announcement from before the recess. Carlisle fetched Hirsch from the hallway, and a few moments later, Hirsch was re-sworn in and seated on the witness stand, awaiting whatever questions Brunelle was about to pose to him.

"Thank you for returning, Mr. Hirsch," Brunelle began. "We just have a few very specific questions for you, okay?"

"Okay," Hirsch agreed.

"It has been suggested," Brunelle started, "that shortly before his murder, your son told you he had a 'solution' regarding the school children across the street. Is that true?"

"A solution?" Hirsch asked. "What does that mean?"

"I suspect it means killing them," Brunelle answered. "Did Caleb tell you shortly before his murder that he was going to kill a bunch of school children?"

Hirsch frowned deeply, almost a scowl. "No. Caleb did not say anything of the sort to me. Not ever."

Brunelle smiled. "Thank you, Mr. Hirsch. No further questions."

"Cross-examination, Ms. Edwards?" Judge Doyle inquired.

"Yes, Your Honor." Edwards practically jumped out of her seat. She stormed around her counsel table and far too close to the witness stand. Hell hath no fury like a defense attorney caught in a lie.

"Your son was a paranoid schizophrenic, wasn't he?" she demanded. No more kid gloves.

"He suffered from a mild form of schizophrenia, paranoid type," Hirsch answered carefully, "which was manageable with medications."

"He had paranoid delusions, didn't he?" Edwards wasn't going to be deterred.

"A few," Hirsch admitted. "But that was why he was seeing Dr. Young."

"He thought people were following him, didn't he?"

"No, not anymore," Hirsch said, his irritation starting to show.

"He wouldn't use his phone because he thought people were monitoring him, isn't that right?"

Hirsch scowled at Edwards. "I don't know anything about the phone. We had a standing lunch date every month. We talked in person."

Edwards didn't really care about the phone. "And he thought those children across the street were all in on it, didn't he?"

"No," Hirsch barked. "No, he did not think that."

"He was suffering from a paranoid delusion that school children were part of a plot against him and he was going to kill them for it, right?"

"No, that's not right," Hirsch insisted, his face turning red.

"In the days leading up to his death," Edwards was almost yelling, "he was obsessed with those children and that's why he was going to kill them all."

"No! No, you're wrong!" Hirsch shouted. "In the days leading up to his murder, his thoughts were lucid and cogent. He was thinking about how caterpillars turn into butterflies and wondering whether he could do that someday too!"

That was weirdly specific, Brunelle thought. He looked to Carlisle, whose expression mirrored his. He looked to Edwards who had turned and was looking back at him. He thought for a moment, double-checking his recollection of all the evidence and how it all fit together,. Then he nodded to Edwards. "Let me redirect."

Edwards's eyebrows shot up. "You want me to stop? Right now?"

"You can recross," Brunelle told her. "Let me redirect."

"Uh, counsel?" Judge Doyle called down from the bench. "This isn't how we do the order of questioning. It's not a negotiation."

"Do you trust me?" Brunelle asked Edwards.

Edwards closed her eyes and shook her head. But she did trust him. "No further questions," she went ahead and said. "For now."

She returned reluctantly to her seat and Brunelle took her place in front of Hirsch.

"When we met in my office the day after your son was murdered," Brunelle recalled, "you told me you only saw Caleb once a month when you had a standing lunch date with him. Do you remember that?"

Hirsch hesitated, his eyes darting slightly under tired lids. "Yes, that's right."

"When you testified at the beginning of the trial," Brunelle continued, "you told the jury that you were scheduled to have that lunch date a few days after his murder. His death. Do you remember that?"

"That's also right," Hirsch admitted.

"And it appears that everyone agrees Caleb wasn't using his phone in the weeks prior to his death," Brunelle recounted. "And yet you were just able to tell us with a great deal of specificity exactly what Caleb's thoughts were in the days immediately before his death."

There wasn't a question there. And Hirsch didn't deny any of it anyway. Brunelle took a step toward Hirsch and asked the question.

"Where is the journal, Mr. Hirsch?"

Hirsch just sat there, a father deer in the headlights.

"You took it from under the bed after I told you what the defense was going to be," Brunelle knew. "Where is it?"

Hirsch still didn't answer.

Brunelle slammed his fist down on the witness stand. "Where is Caleb's journal!" he shouted.

"In my car!" Hirsch shrieked as he recoiled from Brunelle's blow. Then, after a moment of wild-eyed panic, he dropped his head into his hands and started sobbing. "It's in my car. Oh God, it's in my car."

* * *

The bailiff put the jurors into the jury room. The judge probably should have left during the resultant recess as well, but he wasn't about to miss this. Hirsch gave Chen his car keys and Chen returned with the journal. Brunelle laid it on the prosecution table and he, Carlisle, Chen, and Edwards huddled around to read it.

There were certainly references to caterpillars and butterflies but they gave way to less placid imagery. Something happened. The meds probably needed to be adjusted, but it was going to be days before Caleb saw Dr. Young again. Days before he saw his father again. So, the entries turned paranoid. They turned dark. They turned violent. They turned to the students of Longfellow Elementary School.

Carlisle pointed at the page. "This is the last entry. It's from the night before the shooting." Even she wasn't saying 'murder' anymore.

Tomorrow is the day. Tomorrow I will show them I know. Tomorrow I will show them they won't get away with it. They took their innocence away from those children, not me. They recruited them into the war, not me. The blood will be on their hands, not mine.

I don't know if I can trust Zoey. I want to. But if they could get to children, they could get to her. I will tell her what I'm going to do. If she's with them she'll try to stop me. That's how I'll know I'm right. That's how I'll know I have to do it. I will do it. She'll have to kill me to stop me. And she won't do that. No matter how much they got to her, she won't do that.

"Was I right to trust you?" Edwards asked Brunelle.

He nodded. He knew what he needed to do. It was a necessity.

"Your Honor," Brunelle called out as he turned around to face the judge. "The State moves to dismiss this case."

EPILOGUE

Brunelle stared out at the city skyline, the lights twinkling in the evening rain. He was going to miss that view.

"Still thinking about the Addison case?" Casey hobbled up behind him. She was getting around pretty well on her crutches by then.

Brunelle wasn't thinking about the Addison case at all. But he decided he'd rather talk about that than his actual thoughts. "Yeah." He kept his eyes on the city lights.

Casey balanced herself to put a hand on his shoulder. "You did the right thing. It never feels good to lose, but in a way, you didn't. Your job is to seek justice under the law, and that's what you did. That's a win too."

Brunelle nodded. He knew that already. "Thanks."

There was a pause as Brunelle tried to hang onto his quiet thoughts and Casey hesitated before speaking again.

"You'd be a good dad," she said suddenly. Then, with a nervous laugh, she added, "You know, if that ever happens."

Brunelle knew he needed to turn around then. He would have taken Casey by the hands, but she would have dropped her crutches and fallen to the floor. He settled for a hand on her arm. "I'm not so sure," he said. "I saw what Hirsch's father did. I understand why he did it. Hell, I almost did worse to the guy who ran you over. But those are the wrong reasons."

Casey touched his face. "That's why you'd be a good dad. You understand why he did it, but you still know it was wrong."

Brunelle didn't have a reply.

"You're a good man, David Brunelle," Casey insisted.

Brunelle turned back to look at his city, and everything he'd learned over the years about the people who lived in it.

Even himself.

Especially himself.

"I don't know if there is such a thing," he told her, "but it's worth trying."

                              END

THE DAVID BRUNELLE LEGAL THRILLERS
Presumption of Innocence
Tribal Court
By Reason of Insanity
A Prosecutor for the Defense
Substantial Risk
Corpus Delicti
Accomplice Liability
A Lack of Motive
Missing Witness
Diminished Capacity
Devil's Plea Bargain
Homicide in Berlin
Premeditated Intent
Alibi Defense
Defense of Others
Necessity

THE TALON WINTER LEGAL THRILLERS
Winter's Law
Winter's Chance
Winter's Reason
Winter's Justice
Winter's Duty
Winter's Passion

THE RAIN CITY LEGAL THRILLERS
Burden of Proof

ABOUT THE AUTHOR

Stephen Penner is an author, artist, and attorney from Seattle. He draws on his extensive experience as a criminal trial attorney to write several different series of legal thrillers.

The *David Brunelle Legal Thrillers* feature Seattle homicide D.A. David Brunelle and a recurring cast of cops, defense attorneys, and forensic experts. The *Talon Winter Legal Thrillers* star tough-as-nails Tacoma criminal defense attorney Talon Winter. And the *Rain City Legal Thrillers* deliver the adventures of attorney Daniel Raine and his unlikely partner, real estate agent/private investigator Rebecca Sommers.

Stephen is also the author of the *Maggie Devereaux Paranormal Mysteries*, recounting the exploits of an American graduate student in the magical Highlands of Scotland, and several other stand-alone works.

For more information, please visit *www.stephenpenner.com*.

Printed in Great Britain
by Amazon

24156372R00130